Your Friends Came to See Me

—Book 2—

Dying to Be Heard

D1598193

DL Benning

Your Friends Came to See Me

—Book 2—

Dying to Be Heard

Featuring Investigative Medium Lynn Monroe

DL Benning

Printed in the United States of America

First Printing, 2023

ISBN: 978-1-953640-18-5 (paperback)
ISBN: 978-1-953640-19-2 (Kindle edition)
Library of Congress Control Number: 2023909023

Published by McCrady Park Books, an imprint of A Page Beyond, Fishers, Indiana.

This book is a work of fiction, channeled from the Other Side by a self-taught medium. Any resemblance to persons living or dead is either coincidence or confirmation.

Table of Contents

—Chapter 1—
Here We Go Again

My call that morning with Captain Simon of the Ford Heights Police Department had been brief. Still, it would dominate my whole day. Captain Simon wanted me to use my skills as a medium to solve more cold cases in his department's backlog. But could I really do this again? I hadn't channeled any new messages in months, since we'd closed the decades-old murder cases of four young women. And now they'd identified eight more victims, with characteristics and circumstances like the ones from before. Eight! My heart sank at the thought of those young women, their lives taken too early, their families in anguish all these years.

As I laid my phone down on the counter, a faint whiff of cigarette smoke caused my nose to scrunch up. None of the windows were supposed to be open, but since neither my husband, Sam, nor I smoked, the smell had to be coming from outside. I took a few steps forward, closed my eyes, and sniffed the air again, trying to locate the source of the offensive odor. I was surprised by the sudden mental image of a rough-looking young woman taking a long drag from a cigarette. Her name formed in my mind just as unexpectedly: *Polly.*

Polly didn't say anything. She just looked at me coolly, as if sizing me up. There was no malice in her stare, but no warmth either. She struck me as someone who was slow to trust others, someone to whom the world had not been kind. She finished her cigarette, lit another one, and walked away.

Sam came into the kitchen then, just as I opened my eyes. He stopped short when he saw the worry in my face. "You okay? You look like you just saw a ghost," he joked.

"Actually," I said, "you're not far off. I just spoke to Captain Simon. He wants to see me tomorrow about some more cold-case files. And I think I just met one of the victims."

"Here we go again," Sam sighed. He was always supportive of me and came to respect my work, although he had initially shrugged it off as "that New Age shit" he didn't really believe in. He had seemed relieved when my investigation of the Ford Heights murders came to an end. Our dining room was better suited to dinner parties, he'd said, than to seances and interviews with the dead. Honestly, he had a point. I studied him for a moment to see if he was exasperated with me for opening myself back up to medium work. He gave me a quick wink. I appreciated his confidence in me.

***

Just as the day had been full of self-doubt and worry, the night was a restless one for me. No matter what I tried, I just could not fall asleep. Finally, I grabbed my pillow and blanket and tried to leave the room quietly. The floorboard creaked, and Sam asked, "You can't sleep?"

"No, I can't sleep. See you in the morning."

"Okay," he mumbled.

I made my way to the den to try to sleep on the couch. As soon as I closed my eyes, a black-and-white scene started playing in my head. Cornstalks whipped past my field of vision. I quickly opened my eyes. "What was that?" I wondered out loud, shaking my head.

I felt my heart start beating fast. I took a deep breath and closed my eyes again. I heard little girls giggling. They were in the field, running through the dried cornstalks. I could not see their faces. But I could feel them and hear them very clearly. Their voices sounded young.

"Yes, Sam," I whispered to myself, looking up to the ceiling, "*here we go again*. I guess it *is* time for me to get involved with more cold cases." And with that statement, I drifted off to sleep.

When I woke up, Sam had already left for work. He had left me a note wishing me luck and reminding me I was doing the right thing. I smiled as I read it. I folded the note in half and slipped it into my pants pocket. I would need that reminder today.

I sat down for my morning meditation practice. My practice included setting my intention for the day, morning prayers, and always a note of gratitude. As I sat enjoying the solitude, the black-and-white movie with the girls started playing again in my mind. I was sure it was a message of some sort and that more information would come to me when I was ready. As I was ending my practice, I added a prayer asking for the most benevolent outcome with Captain Simon today.

As I drove from my north-Chicago suburb to the Ford Heights police station, my mind wandered back to when I had made this drive so many times to care for my elderly Aunt Mary and her horrible husband, Fred, in their final years. Even after my dear Aunt Mary's death, the responsibility of looking after Fred fell solely to me, his reluctant power-of-attorney. I dreaded every visit to the nursing home in Ford Heights, every "outing" to lawyers' offices and doctors' appointments. After each of these excursions, Fred would insist we stop by the shuttered home of his long-deceased mother. There he would walk the perimeter of the house, meticulously checking locks and pacing the property line. This particular ritual was always unsettling to me, even more than the never-ending complaints and occasional accusations hurled in my direction. For a couple years, I'd chalked it up to my resentment toward this bitter, hateful man and the way he had treated my beloved Aunt Mary. But then I met Nina.

Nina was the local psychic. I'd visited her in hopes of finding a guide to help me develop my meditation practice and channeling abilities. At the time, I used my gift for journaling inspirational messages. Nothing more. Nina changed all that. She told me my uncle had committed horrible crimes, and that I would need to use my medium gift to uncover the truth. My confusion turned to panic as I saw plainly, standing next to Nina, a woman from the past, covered in mud and asking for my help. I didn't believe Nina when she told me I would hone my skills as a medium, confront my uncle, confirm his crimes with DNA evidence, and write a book about the experience. But that is exactly what happened over the four years since that fateful meeting.

Booking that session with Nina had changed my whole life for the better. I paused and questioned the truth of that sentence. *Yes*, I was convinced, *for the better*! Would Sam agree with that? I thought he would. I smiled to myself, my head nodding along with my thoughts.

As my drive continued, I marveled at the magic and the natural order of the universe. Trying through my human brain to comprehend the divine timing of all the meetings and people who showed up in such wonderful and purposeful ways to help me. Divine intervention was the only explanation, however implausible it all seemed.

There were still times I would wonder, *Did all this really happen, or was it a dream?* Alone in the car, I reassured myself aloud, "Yes, this really happened." What a wild ride it had been! This was the stuff movies are made of. *Maybe someday*, I thought, *but right now my focus needs to be on these new cases. Stay in the present,* I reminded myself. Then, with a chuckle, *Or in this case, the past.*

I arrived at the police station and put my car in park. For a moment, I pondered all the mysteries held within the building. *Would I be able to solve eight more of them?* I pulled out my note from Sam and read it to myself. Then, I took a deep breath and got out of the car.

Summoning a bit of courage, I whispered to myself, "Showtime!" and walked into the police station with as much confidence as I could muster.

Inside the police station, Captain Simon greeted me and introduced a young, plainclothes detective who would brief me on the cases. Captain Simon addressed this young man only as "Bradley," and I wasn't sure if that was his first name or his last name.

I extended my hand to shake his, "Nice to meet you, Officer … Bradley …?" hoping he would fill in whichever name was missing.

"Yes," he answered without shaking my hand. "This way."

I followed the two policemen to an unused office. It was a little room and dimly lit, although one of the walls was made mostly of glass. There was a small, dark metal table with three mismatched leather chairs around it. There were a few windows high up on the wall, near the ceiling. I could see daylight shining through. I noticed several cardboard file boxes stacked in one corner. Captain Simon gestured to a well-worn desk chair and explained that he would be just down the hall should we have any questions. He nodded to Bradley and took his leave.

Officer Bradley produced eight manila folders, stacking them on the small table. "These are unsolved cases from the 1950s, '60s, and '70s," he explained. "The victims are all women who were from Ford Heights or whose bodies were found within our jurisdiction. Or at least, what *was* our jurisdiction at the time they were found." He took a long look at me, seemingly annoyed. "I guess a lot's changed since then."

I imagined that the 1970s fell under the category of "ancient history" for someone as young as Officer Bradley. But I nodded, even while my stomach was doing flip-flops in anticipation of what those folders might reveal.

"Do you think my uncle was responsible for these murders?" I asked.

"Not necessarily," Officer Bradley said with a shrug. "He was a strangler, right? Some of these women, maybe. Others? Different M.O.s. Not all of them young, some not from the area. A couple Jane Does. No ties to the boarding house or the forest preserve or your uncle specifically."

When Officer Bradley mentioned the forest preserve, I bristled. My uncle had left all four of his victims in the woods there. Three of the women had lived in the same boarding house, though not at the same time. The young women had all visited me, in spirit, to tell me their stories and ask for my help in uncovering the truth about my uncle.

Officer Bradley continued, "Although, I think that old detective must have questioned your uncle about every woman who turned up dead or went missing for the next several years."

Despite my nerves, I couldn't help but smile at the mention of "that old detective," Detective Tom Roman. In life, he had been relentless—but unsuccessful—in pursuing my Uncle Fred for the four, nearly-identical murders. In death, he had stepped forward as a guide to help me collect evidence. It was Detective Roman who insisted I contact the police department to bring official closure to the cases. His spirit couldn't rest until justice was served.

"There's a lot of notes in these files about your uncle," Bradley explained, "even where we didn't see a connection to the case. We started looking through them after you—after we closed those other four cases. When the Captain saw the name Fred Federoski, he thought maybe you could help us."

"I can try," I replied.

"I guess the best thing to do is just walk through these, one at a time, and see if anything … um … speaks to you?" Officer Bradley said.

At first, I didn't realize it was a question. Bradley probably hadn't spent a lot of his law enforcement career consulting mediums about cold cases. In fairness, I didn't have a lot of experience with this process either. I hoped my earlier successes hadn't been a fluke.

"Yes, I think that would be a good place to start," I agreed, hoping I sounded more confident than I felt.

Officer Bradley opened the first folder and began to recount the gruesome details from handwritten field notes, occasionally sharing a crime-scene photo that had turned brittle with age. The young woman had been viciously attacked in an alleyway. The motive appeared to have been robbery, since both her wallet and her birthstone ring were missing.

Next, Bradley opened one of the cardboard file boxes marked EVIDENCE in handwritten Sharpie. He put on some latex gloves and carefully removed photographs, bits of fabric, and some crumpled paper that had been soiled with dirt and blood. The young detective read the description of each item from the official inventory list.

"Anything?" he asked.

"No, but could I sit with these items for a moment?" I offered.

"Sure, I'll give you a minute. Just don't *touch* anything but the case file, okay?"

"Yes, of course," I said.

"Okay. Um … you want a cup of coffee or something?" he asked uncertainly.

"Yeah, that'd be great." I was grateful for the gesture, although it felt like he made the offer out of habit rather than genuine hospitality.

He took off the gloves and disappeared out the door, leaving me alone with the items. I forced myself to look at each piece, steadying my breath and setting my intention to honor any information that revealed itself. I held the case file in my hands, connecting my energy to it, and concentrated on the victim's name, Barbara.

At one point, my gaze wandered out past the office door, into the open area of the police station. I felt Detective Roman's presence, but I didn't know where he was exactly. In my head, I whispered, *I feel you. Where are you?* My attention went to the right corner of the large room, to an empty, gray leather chair. Yep, there he was, his aura gentle and reassuring. I smiled at the empty chair, hoping no one noticed.

After several minutes, Officer Bradley returned with a Styrofoam cup full of hot coffee. Captain Simon was right behind him, with his own coffee mug and a hopeful expression. Seeing my half-shrug, he put his hand on my forearm and asked, "Lynn, do you need to take a break?"

Need a break? I thought to myself, *I need to get out of here and get these horrible images out of my head!*

"If we stop now, I may not come back. It's a lot, seeing these pictures and knowing what happened to this poor girl," I admitted. "Nothing here connected for me, but maybe there's something else that will."

Despite my urge to run away, I felt very cared for by Captain Simon. He was a kind man who seemed motivated to bring closure to these long-forgotten cases. I wondered whether I would be able to help him.

As the detective read through each remaining case, I listened for the name Polly or any connection to a cornfield. I scanned the old photographs for a face that matched the wary, chain-smoking woman who'd appeared to me the day before. None of them matched the visions I'd had, and my heart sank a little more with each passing hour.

Listening to the details of each of the crimes was overwhelming for me. Each time the detective described another woman's case, I felt sick to my stomach. I shook my head, closed my eyes, and said a little prayer for the victim and her family. With every new box of physical evidence, I hoped for flashes of insight that didn't come. *Who had these women been, and why wouldn't they show themselves to me?*

Detective Roman sat with me in spirit, listening intently as we reviewed each case. He would nod his head and smile at me, encouraging me to relax a bit. Knowing he was close by made me feel safe. Occasionally he would whisper, "You can do this, Lynn. Know I am with you. We are all with you."

All with me? I thought. I didn't hear any words, but a sense of reassurance washed over me. In my medium practice, I had learned to trust these feelings and not reason them away.

The meeting at the police station lasted nearly five hours. As Officer Bradley closed the box on the last case—a Jane Doe who'd been stabbed in a roadside motel—Captain Simon returned. He didn't speak right away. Silence makes me uncomfortable, but I fought my discomfort and kept quiet.

After a long pause, the captain looked at me very intently and then back at the stack of case files. He said, "Lynn, we need you to help us. Solving these cold cases will help us provide closure to families that's long overdue. What commitment can you give us right now to helping with these investigations?"

Commitment? I thought to myself. My eyes went to the empty chair. Detective Roman nodded to me with a wink.

"Commitment, uh …, yes." I cleared my throat to speak louder and more confidently. It didn't work. "I, I … I will help you. I will do my best."

He said, "I can make office space for you here, if you like."

Here? I thought. *Please, don't make me drive all the way down here every week.* I quickly replied, "I think it would be best for me to work at home. After all, energy is energy," I joked. No one laughed. I am sure they didn't get the sentiment.

Captain Simon seemed confused but pressed on. "Well, we can't let the evidence leave the station. But we can keep the boxes in this room for the time being. Call Bradley here if you'd like to take another look." At this, Officer Bradley managed a weak and weary smile.

"So, I can go now?" I asked, perhaps a little too eagerly. I realized I was famished after a full day at the police station, with bitter coffee to drink and only my own thoughts to chew on. I left in defeat, unable to solve even the minor mystery of Officer Bradley's name.

—Chapter 2—
The Backyard Discovery

I decided to take a slight detour to grab a sandwich before getting into the heavy highway traffic. In doing so, I realized I was just a few blocks away from where my Uncle Fred's mother had lived. Although that place gave me the creeps, I felt unexpectedly pulled toward it. I suspected this was a message from my spirit guides. Reluctantly, I turned away from the highway, toward the abandoned house that had once belonged to Alma Federoski.

On the way there, I wondered how I would feel being on that property again. It had been a long time since my last trip there, when my friends and I had conducted a fruitless search for evidence of Fred's crimes. I chuckled as I remembered Jeren, the off-duty cop who'd gone with us, kicking in the kitchen door with her cowboy boots. But then my thoughts gave way to what we'd found inside—a hoarder's chaotic jumble of trinkets and trash—and what we hadn't: the mementos Fred had saved from each of his crimes.

I slowed my car as I approached the property. I pulled off the street and parked in the lot next to the house. I kept the engine running, since I didn't plan to get more than a couple steps from the car. It was getting dark, and the neighborhood seemed sketchy at night.

Just then, my phone rang.

"Hey, Sam," I answered.

"Are you still at the police station?" he asked, concerned.

"I left there about thirty minutes ago. Stopped for a bite. Now I'm over at Fred's mother's house."

Sam was confused. "Why on earth would you head over there at this hour?"

"I don't know. I felt like I needed to come here again, so I did." My explanation sounded silly when I said it out loud.

Sam said, "Seriously, Lynn, it's getting dark, and it's not safe for you to be there now. Get in the car and come home."

"It's fine. I'll be fine," I said, trying to convince both of us. I did wonder if it was safe for me to be there. I knew I shouldn't stay too long.

Sam pleaded with me to come home. "Lynn, it will be dark soon. I don't like you being there by yourself. There could be squatters living there." Then, remembering why he'd called in the first place, he added, "Hey, what'd you find out from the police?"

"No strong connections to Fred in any of the cases, so that was a relief. But the bad news is that I wasn't able to connect to the cases, either. I think I have more work to do."

"Then come on home and do it," he urged me.

Hearing the concern in his voice, I said, "I need a minute here. I'll leave before sunset."

"Good." He sounded relieved. "Call me when you're on the road."

Something was drawing me to stay there. I had learned to trust these feelings. I couldn't leave. I walked around the backyard. Every few steps, I would stop, close my eyes, and ask, *What do I need to know? I am here, I want to help. Is there a message for me?*

A strong energy suddenly filled my consciousness. Instantly, I knew I was being visited by my Uncle Fred and his creepy mother, Alma. They weren't happy I was on their turf. I ordered them to leave me alone, and they left as quickly as they had appeared. I took a deep breath and shook my shoulders to clear my mind again.

I heard, "Ask me?" and felt two eyes hiding in a dark closet.

"Who are you?" I asked silently.

The voice was soft and young. I heard a T, but the rest of the word was muffled.

"Sorry, I can't quite understand you."

"My name is Teddy. Short for Theodora."

"Welcome, Teddy."

"Hi," she said shyly.

"What do you have to tell me, Teddy?"

"I would like to tell you my story" She seemed nervous and was looking around her. She blurted out, "I'm hiding."

"Why are you hiding?" I asked.

"It is a secret," she whispered.

"A secret from who?" I asked curiously.

"Him. *You know.*" She looked around nervously. "That man, Fred. I saw him. I saw him bury a girl. I lived next door. I saw him drag her into the backyard and bury her. I was looking down from my roof, over there." She pointed to a two-story building on a nearby lot. "I liked to go out onto the roof to see the moon and the stars. I heard them laughing and talking. And then it got quiet. Really quiet. I had watched them for a few months. They were lovers. Secret lovers. No one was supposed to know about them."

"Why was it a secret?"

"It was forbidden by Fred's mother. She didn't want them to be together."

"Really?" I asked curiously.

"Really! She was a mean old woman. I was selling recipe cookbooks for our church once. I asked her to buy one from me. She slammed the door in my face. Fred was nice to me, though. Sometimes he would bring me jellybean candies in a little, white, paper bag. He would tease me and say I was getting taller every time he saw me. I liked him at first."

"At first?"

"Yes, at first, until I saw what he did to her."

"What he did to who?" I said, surprised.

She hesitated and quietly said, "I am afraid to talk to you."

"Why are you afraid? I want to help you. I'm working with the detectives here to solve eight cold cases. I need your help to tell the truth. Will you help me?"

"Are you sure you should tell the truth?" she asked.

It was a good question, and one I'd asked myself many times.

"Yes, I am," I tried to sound more convincing than I was feeling.

Teddy continued, "You know what happens to women who tell the truth? Do you? He kills them. I have seen this happen twice. He choked them and broke their necks. Then he dug holes in his mother's backyard. He put their bodies in the holes. Right there, by the canoe. He laid them right next to each other. His mother helped him shovel the dirt. They both scare me. When he gave me candy after that, I threw it away. I was afraid to eat it."

"Tell me more, Teddy. I am here to protect you. Did you tell anyone else?"

"No! No one."

"Why not?" I asked her.

"Well, I was on the roof, and I wasn't supposed to be. My parents would have punished me and not let me go up there again. But I loved the moon. The dark sky and the stars. Oh, the stars! You could see them so clearly some nights. Ford Heights was a quiet town at night."

"Teddy, what else should I know?"

"The story has a lot of twists and turns. Are you sure you're up for it?"

"I am sure. Thank you for helping me. I need all the help I can get."

"Thank you."

I sensed she was blushing. Slowly, I started to see her in my mind. She was a small, thin girl, with dark-framed eyeglasses and crooked front teeth. Teddy had a face full of freckles and a tomboy vibe.

"How long did you live here?" I continued.

"Most of my life. My parents worked hard. They both worked. I was alone a lot. I had one brother. He was not home a lot. He had a truck and a girlfriend. Well, a lot of girlfriends, really," she giggled.

"What did you like about the night, the moon, and the stars?"

"I loved them all. I loved science. I studied hard in school. I dreamed of becoming an astronaut taking a rocket ship to the moon. That'd be fun. I think they do that one day, don't they?"

I stopped and asked cautiously, "Wait, Teddy, how old are you?"

"I am thirteen. My mother told me not to talk to Fred, or his mother, or his sister. She said they were not good people. Mother said, 'We just need to mind our own business.' I think my parents were afraid of them, too."

"Really, why?" I asked.

"Because they were sneaky. They were always looking over their shoulders. Fred was always looking around the property, especially where he buried those women's bodies. He covered them with a lot of twigs and branches. But I saw what they did, him and his mother," she said, the words rushing out.

Teddy continued, "They didn't come outside much. Their curtains were always closed. I was not allowed on their sidewalk if Fred's mother saw me. She would stare at me and chase me away. One time, she was sweeping the front steps, and I was walking by. I put my head down when I saw her, but she yelled after me. She was waving her broom at me and yelling, 'I said, get out of here.'"

"I've been told she was mean," I agreed, grateful never to have met the woman. Then, I got a sick feeling in my stomach. "Teddy, did they know you saw them? Did they hurt you, too?"

"No, I was killed in a car accident many years later."

"How old were you?"

"I was forty-two."

"That seems young. Did you have a good life?"

"I did! I sure did. You know, they did go to the moon several times."

"Yes." I smiled, "They sure did. Teddy, I would like to come back to you for help. Is that okay?"

"Yes, it is very okay with me."

I kept my eyes closed, squeezing them tight. I was trying to hold onto the conversation for as long as I could. I took out my notebook and wrote down all I could remember.

When I looked up from my note pad, I noticed a firefly—we call them *lightning bugs* in the Midwest—floating up from some tall, thick grass near the property line. I stood there for a moment, hoping to see it again. It was not uncommon to see a lighting bug that time of night, and I always loved seeing them. It always signified for me that summer was starting soon. In this case, it also reminded me that night was falling, and I needed to leave. But I couldn't move from the spot.

As if to reward my stillness, another lightning bug lit up over the tall grass. And then another one. And suddenly, right before my eyes, there were hundreds of fireflies, floating up and down in the tall grass. It took my breath away! I got the sense that they were playing a song, a melody of some sort, with their movement. They danced up and down like synchronized swimmers. I was enthralled. I lost my voice and began to cry. I dropped to my knees and whispered, "Who's here? Who's here? I am here to help you."

I heard several voices respond, "Tell our story. Tell our story." The voices kept repeating, "Tell our story."

"Yes, I will! I will tell your story. I will. Thank you for trusting me to share it. I won't stop until I do. I promise. The world will hear your stories!"

I was overcome by emotion, wishing Sam were there to witness what was happening. *Sam! He's going to be worried if I don't call soon.* I walked quickly back to my car, still running and ready in the adjacent lot.

Inside the car, I took a deep breath and tried to calm myself down. Out loud I said, "Thank you. Thank you for trusting me, for choosing me. I honor you. All of you." I looked back one more time before pulling away. The lighting bugs were still there, dancing to what seemed like a beautiful melody I couldn't hear, but one I could feel in my soul.

I drove home. My mind was going crazy with thoughts and emotions. When I called Sam, my words tumbled out so quickly that he couldn't make sense of them.

"Lynn, are you in the car? Are you okay? Can you drive?"

"Yes, yes, I can drive" I said nodding my head as if he could see it. "Oh, Sam. There are more women. They are buried there on Alma's property." I continued, "I have to help them. I have to help them." Through tears, I recounted the story of the lightning bugs and the melody they seemed to be playing.

Sam listened quietly to my rambling. I am certain I wasn't making any sense.

After a moment, he said, "Maybe you should just call the captain and let him handle this."

"What? Him, handle this? No, I am handling this," I said sharply. I knew he was just concerned about my wellbeing and probably not ready to have our lives turned upside down again. I softened my tone. "I have to see this through. You know I do."

Sam was silent for a moment. Then he said, quietly, "I know. I know you do."

—Chapter 3—
Calling for Backup

I was exhausted by the time I got home. On the way inside, I nearly slipped on a plastic-wrapped magazine that had been tossed into our driveway. Stooping to pick it up, I recognized the masthead. We hadn't subscribed to *Chicago Living Magazine* in years. Maybe Sam had renewed in hopes of finding new jazz clubs we could visit.

I walked into the house much later than planned, but Sam was waiting in the kitchen for me with a glass of Scotch and a plate of leftovers.

"So, what's your plan?" he asked.

"I need to go back to the house," I said. Then, seeing the alarm on his face, I added, "with my friends, in the daytime."

Sam's tension eased a bit. "Your friend from work and her neighbor, the cop?"

"Yes, Sadie and Jeren. I'll talk to Sadie tomorrow and see when we can all make the trip." I paused, lost for a moment in thought. "It's weird, though, Sam. None of the police files triggered any visits or visions. Just … nothing. And there was no file on Polly, and nothing related to a cornfield."

"What cornfield?" Sam asked.

"Last night, I kept having visions of a cornfield. From the perspective of a child, like I was running through the rows of stalks. I'm sure it has something to do with Polly," I explained.

"Well, give it time, Lynn," Sam said reassuringly. "I'm sure you'll figure this out." I appreciated his confidence in me almost as much as I appreciated the glass of Scotch.

"Oh, hey," I said, suddenly remembering. "Did you sign us up for *Chicago Living* again? This was in the driveway when I came home."

Sam shook his head but reached for the magazine. "Maybe they're hoping we'll renew if they send us a freebie." He tore open the plastic wrapper, and his jaw went slack.

"What is it?" I asked.

He turned the magazine around to show me the front cover. On it was an artist's sketch of a young man, sporting handcuffs and a James Dean-style haircut, behind a headline that read: *"Paroled? Yes. Exonerated? Maybe: Reexamining* the 'Starved Rock Killer' Case After 59 Years in Prison. Was he innocent after all?"

It took a moment to form my next thought. "Oh, my God, Sam! Do you think Fred could have been responsible for the Starved Rock murders?"

"That seems like a long shot," he said. But he didn't sound very convincing. "Maybe read the article before you jump to conclusions?"

"Tomorrow," I promised. "For now, I need a bath and some time to decompress."

***

The next day at work, I briefed Sadie on my disappointing performance at the police station, my encounter with Teddy and the fireflies, and the mysterious appearance of the magazine in our driveway. "Anyway, I think it's time to get the band back together to search the old house again. There's more to this story. I can feel it," I concluded.

Sadie was excited. "Let's call Jeren and see if she's free this weekend!"

We made the call, only to learn that Jeren could not help us. She had broken a bone in her foot, for which she had been issued an orthopedic boot and assigned to desk duty. "I'm not allowed to kick in any more doors for a while," she joked.

Sadie and I both chuckled, remembering our last trip to the Federoski house. Jeren had arrived wearing a holstered gun and cowboy boots, the latter of which she used to kick the door in when all my keys proved to be useless. Thankfully, the gun hadn't been necessary.

Jeren suggested that her friend Beth join us instead. Beth, she explained, was a psychic who occasionally helped solve cases in Jeren's jurisdiction. Jeren assured me she would brief Beth about the case.

"But, listen," she cautioned, "you can't go busting in the house this time. I won't be with you, and you don't know who might have taken up residence in an abandoned place like that."

"Well, then we can't get in. I don't have a key anymore," I admitted. "I mean, not that any of mine worked, anyway. But I handed everything over to Fred's niece after his funeral. His sister's kid. That would have been her grandmother's house, so it's hers now."

"Can she give you a key?" Jeren asked.

"I don't know. She lives out of state, and I really don't want to drag her into all this. I'll see what I can do."

"Okay, in the meantime, I'll get Beth up to speed and get you two connected. Sound good?"

"Thanks, Jeren, and I hope you're back in the right kind of boot soon!"

Sadie pressed the end-call button and looked over at me, a bit disheartened.

"Now what?" she asked.

"I guess we wait until we have a key and a chaperone and a plan," I offered, acutely aware of my own impatience. Waiting has never been my favorite.

I debated for a few days about how to open the conversation with Margie, Fred's niece. I had intentionally kept her out of the loop on her late uncle's criminal activity. The less she knew about him, the better she'd sleep at night.

My deliberations were cut short when Margie called unexpectedly. She wanted me to know that the house had been condemned. Margie had sold the lot to a local developer, and the house would be leveled soon. I knew it was bittersweet for her. Her grandfather had built the house in 1935, and the house held many family memories. For me, it represented something else entirely. I thanked Margie for calling and promised I would go say goodbye to the house for her.

Sadie, Beth, and I met at the property that Saturday. The backyard was overgrown with weeds. The garage roof looked like it had finally collapsed. The windows and doors were boarded up with plywood that had black and orange numbers spray painted on it.

We knew we couldn't enter the house but remained optimistic. Our goal was to find any evidence of the backyard graves Teddy mentioned. Still, we were technically trespassing, so we vowed to leave the property undisturbed and to play dumb if anyone asked why we were there.

Beth and I clicked immediately. She brought sketches on a yellow, lined legal pad. Beth walked me to the back of the house with her.

"What do you see?" she asked.

It seemed like a trick question, "Overgrown weeds and trees," I answered.

"No. What do you see by the canoe?"

Canoe, I thought. *What canoe?* I looked around the backyard. On the left side, there was a battered, discarded canoe. It was covered in weeds and fallen tree branches, but I could see it plainly once Beth pointed it out. I had never noticed it before. I closed my eyes and opened them immediately. "Oh my God, there's a body buried there." I looked at her in shock.

She nodded. "How many bodies do you see?"

Of course, I did not physically see them with my eyes. However, in my mind's eye, I could see the remains of four bodies. Quietly, I whispered, "I see three, maybe four."

She nodded, "Yes, there are four bodies buried here, one right next to the other." Then she showed me her notepad, with sketches she'd made before she arrived: the canoe and four bodies.

I felt sick to my stomach. "Oh no," I repeated, "Oh no." I leaned up against the house, feeling my knees starting to buckle. My hopes that I'd put Fred's crimes behind me were crumbling fast. He'd taken the lives of four more women, and they had been right here the whole time.

I looked at the labels on Beth's sketch pad. *P, N, R, X …* Polly. The police wouldn't have had a cold case file on Polly if her body was never found!

Beth continued, "This house has an evil and angry energy attached to it. We need to get finished and out of here quickly today. We don't have much time."

As we walked the property, Beth asked me how well I knew Fred's mother. I shrugged my shoulders and said I'd never met her in person. I explained that she had come to me several times in spirit and seemed angry.

She said, "Very angry. Don't think she just turned a blind eye to all of Fred's activities. She was definitely not an innocent bystander in all of this."

"What do you mean?" I asked, surprised.

"This is a Norman Bates kind of thing."

"Who?"

"From the movie. *Psycho*?" she answered.

I admitted I'd never seen the movie.

"Oh, not important. When Fred's mother didn't like one of his girlfriends, she would give him 'the nod.' Fred knew that meant to get rid of her."

I shuddered. I'd been shown enough scenes from my uncle's sinister past to understand the full impact of Beth's words.

We finished our survey of the overgrown lot, finding nothing on the surface that would prove the existence of the graves. Since the land had been sold, we couldn't disturb the property. But I was determined to unearth the truth, regardless.

The next Monday morning, I called down to the Ford Heights police station and asked to speak with "Bradley."

"May I tell him who's calling?" Karen, the receptionist, asked.

"This is Lynn Monroe," I said, cheerfully. "We're working together on some cold cases."

"I'm sorry, Lynn. He's asked me to take a message if you called," she said.

"I'm sorry I missed him. Can you please ask him to look for an unsolved missing-persons case from the 1960s? The person in question would be named Polly. I don't have a last name just yet."

"Sure thing, sweetie," Karen said. "Anything else?"

"Ask him if it's possible for us to dig up the backyard that used to belong to Fred Federoski. His mother's old place, not his own residence. I believe he'll find Polly's remains there, along with two or three other victims."

"Is that your late uncle? Are you in possession of his property?" Karen clearly remembered my previous work with the department. I was relieved.

"No. I mean, yes, it was my uncle's. But no, I'm not in possession of it. His niece recently sold the place. She didn't say who bought it," I said.

"I'll pass this along," Karen said. Her voice dropped almost to a whisper. "And just between us girls, you might find him in the station if you dropped in, rather than called."

"So, he's avoiding me, then?" I asked.

"That sounds good, Lynn," she said cheerfully, "I'll be sure to pass this information along, and I'm sure you'll be hearing from him soon! Don't be a stranger around the department, okay?"

"Thank you, Karen. I'll plan to visit soon."

I wasn't surprised that Bradley didn't seem to be taking me seriously. Still, I was hurt and disappointed. I didn't have access to the resources he did. And, as much as I hated to admit it, I couldn't solve these cases on my own. I let out a deep sigh, when I noticed the *Chicago Living Magazine* lying on the kitchen counter.

The cover image gave me the creeps. The story was about a man that had been in prison for almost sixty years for killing three Chicagoland women in the early sixties. The article said this was the most heinous crime in Illinois history at the time. Three women, all the wives of influential men, were murdered at Starved Rock State Park while hiking together in the woods.

I shuddered, wondering again if my uncle could have been involved. After all, the timeframe and park setting were in line with some of the murders he committed. But the victims themselves and some of the crime scene details didn't fit his pattern. These women were older than the four victims I'd met through my medium work. And they'd been bludgeoned, rather than strangled. Still, the what-if thoughts ran over and over obsessively in my mind.

I read the magazine article three times, reading each word carefully and looking for clues. The article explained the methods the police used to investigate the crime, including the pressure campaign that resulted in their prime suspect's confession, which he immediately recanted and consistently denied for the next six decades. There was mention of a woman who had held onto information about the murders, waiting to speak up only when she was on her deathbed. There was also information about a specialized lab in Elgin, Illinois, that recovered contaminated DNA evidence with a great deal of accuracy.

I decided to consult my heavenly sources about my uncle's possible involvement in this case. They quickly confirmed that my Uncle Fred was not the murderer. I was relieved. My spirit guides wanted me to know how murder cases were managed in those days, along with some other clues that would spark my curiosity when I was ready to receive more information. Despite my insistence that I was eager for more details right then, my guides reminded me that everything would unfold in divine time. *Be patient*, they advised.

—Chapter 4—
Natalie Speaks

Once a month on the weekends, I work on new blog posts for my spiritual healing practice, The Purple Bridge. Always the procrastinator, I tend to wait until the night before they are due. The hardest part about getting the writing done is sitting down and getting started. Once I do, inspiration always comes to me. Or maybe I need the adrenaline rush of a deadline to spur me into action.

As I began looking through my notes, I felt a presence in the room. There was no one physically there with me. Still, I sensed someone sitting in a chair nearby. This was a common occurrence for the last few years. The more I tuned into my gift, the stronger the messages and sensations came through to me. Curious, I closed my eyes to see who was present. I could not get a clear picture of the woman sitting in the chair, but I recognized the four women standing behind her.

My old friends: M, Carol, Julia, and Agnes. They were the original four women I met when this whole story with my uncle Fred revealed itself to me. He had dated—or been interested in dating—all these beautiful souls. When the relationship faded or his affection wasn't reciprocated, he murdered them. Each one of the women had made contact with me through their spirit selves and shared the details of their lives and deaths.

Staying connected with the women, I noticed four more chairs appear in my mind, next to the one occupied by the nameless woman. Three of the new chairs were empty. My new friend Teddy occupied the fourth one. *Hello*, I said slowly and cautiously to the four chairs. *What have you come to tell me?*

The scene in my mind instantly flashed to the home where Fred had lived with his mother. I followed where the energy was leading me, to the backyard and specifically to the canoe buried in the weeds. *Ok,* I said, *what do you need me to know?*

The new woman spoke to me, "Hi, I am Natalie. I am buried in the second grave, here by the canoe. Can you see me?"

"Not yet," I answered. I was not sure what was coming next. I waited for her to continue.

"Do you see the canoe?"

I nodded. She took a piece of paper and drew a sketch of four bodies buried near the canoe. The bodies would be nothing but bones by now, but it was clear they were human remains. Then Natalie said to me, "Is it okay to talk to you?"

Yes! Yes, it is more than okay. I have been working with the police for the last few years to solve these murders. I am a medium and a truth seeker. I want to bring the truth to light about my uncle's involvement in these cases. I want your families and friends to finally know what happened to each of you.

Natalie continued, "Lynn, my dear, things unfold as they are supposed to. Nothing can be rushed. Everything in this universe happens in divine time. Just perfectly perfect. Do you know what I mean?"

Well, sometimes I do. Most of the time, I just feel behind and rushed. Sometimes I feel good enough, and sometimes I don't.

I felt Natalie smile, "Yes, dear, that is part of being human. Walk with me now." She held out her hand, and in my mind, I followed her. She took me behind the house, where she aimed a flashlight beam onto a rock. The rock had something etched on it. Then she showed me there were four rocks. We walk over to the first one. P – Polly, N – Natalie, R – Ruth, and X.

Who is X, Natalie?

"You will meet her soon," she said.

I nodded. "Okay."

Natalie, I continued, *tell me about you and your life.*

She sighed, "Oh, dear girl. Sit down, and I will tell you."

***

Natalie grew up in a poor neighborhood in Ford Heights. Her mother was a maid in the mayor's home. It was a high-profile, if not lucrative, job. Natalie had dated a few boys in high school. One of the boys she'd hoped to marry, but their relationship didn't last.

After graduation, Natalie found work as a maid in some of the wealthier neighborhoods near Ford Heights. She didn't mind the work, and her customers were generally nice people. The pay was steady. She had plenty of time to spend with her friends.

Natalie relished her freedom. Her style was bold for the times. She wore dark red lipstick, a leather jacket, and brightly colored scarves. She frequented dive bars, where she would drink, smoke, and play pool with the regulars. She never saw herself as especially social, but always felt like she belonged in the seedy, smoke-filled pool halls.

She realized the men in these bars were quick to underestimate a young woman who scrubbed toilets for a living. Natalie would use this to her advantage, hustling guys for money playing pool. Sometimes, they'd get angry. Other times, they'd buy her a drink or invite her to come home with them. Either way, she knew she was playing with fire. She saw it all as an adventure.

Her parents soon tired of her reckless behavior and kicked her out of their house. She stayed with a friend for a few days, but that arrangement wouldn't last long. She needed to find a more permanent place to live.

At the supermarket one day, Natalie found a "Rooms for Rent" flyer on the bulletin board. She took down the phone number and address. When she called the number, an older lady answered. The woman wasn't friendly, but the price was right. There was a bus stop close to the house, which meant Natalie could get to work—and to the bars—easily.

She went by the boarding house that afternoon to check it out. The older woman who answered the door introduced herself as Mrs. W. Even as Mrs. W. invited Natalie in, Natalie thought the older woman seemed uncomfortable. Natalie wondered fleetingly if her leather jacket was a red flag to a boarding house matron, but Natalie saw a few red flags of her own. Her first impression of the home was that it both looked and smelled like her grandmother's house. Roses and mothballs dominated her senses. But the house had none of the warmth of a grandmother. It seemed cold and stale. Unsettling.

Mrs. W. invited Natalie to sit at the kitchen table. She explained the house rules and when the rent was due. The woman seemed distracted, and even a little sad. She provided the information as if she'd repeated it more times than she would have liked. Then Mrs. W. asked Natalie if she had any questions.

"How many people live here?" Natalie asked, trying to sound friendly.

Mrs. W. answered quickly, "A few girls at a time. I have two open rooms. They … moved on recently." The older woman's eyes darted to the right, and she swallowed hard. Natalie wondered whether she was telling the truth, but she pressed on.

"Could I see the open rooms, then?"

The two walked upstairs. Mrs. W. looked over her shoulder frequently to ensure Natalie was still close by. The two available rooms were similar in size and decor. Each room sported frilly, gingham curtains, a twin bed with a chenille bedspread, a small writing desk, and a garbage can. The closets were small, but Natalie didn't have much to fill them with anyway.

"I'll take it," Natalie said.

"You can move in over the weekend," Mrs. W. offered. She wrote down Natalie's personal information and walked her to the door.

The screen door slammed shut after Natalie crossed the threshold. She lit a cigarette on the porch and walked down the stairs to the sidewalk. When she looked back toward the house, she saw Mrs. W. watching her from the window. The landlady eyed both Natalie and the cigarette, stared for several moments, then dropped the curtain. As Natalie walked to the bus stop, she wondered what she had gotten herself into.

The following Saturday, Natalie moved in with just three boxes of clothes and personal items. She closed her door and put away her few belongings. She chuckled at the juxtaposition of her leather jacket hanging on the bedpost, in front of the ruffled curtains. It was a clear sign that she didn't belong there.

There was a soft knock on the door. A pretty, blond girl stood in the hallway. "Hi, I'm Sally!" she said and put her hand out to shake Natalie's.

Natalie reluctantly shook her hand. She'd never met anyone so perky.

"We're going to the dance club tonight, if you'd like to come," Sally chirped.

"Dance club?" Natalie laughed awkwardly, imagining herself at sock hop with a bunch of goodie-two-shoes. "Thanks, but I have other plans."

"Okay. Maybe next week? We go every Saturday night." As she talked, she swayed her body back and forth like she was doing a dance routine.

"Yeah, maybe," Natalie said sarcastically.

Natalie closed the door and sat on the bed. "Oh, God. What did I do?" she said to herself. "I don't belong here, I just don't."

She decided she'd feel more comfortable at one of her regular hangouts. She changed into a white top, slid into her black leather jacket and tied a bright red scarf around her neck. From her closet, she pulled out a pair of brand-new motorcycle boots that zipped up the sides. She added a pop of red lipstick to boost her confidence and headed toward the stairs.

Natalie's new housemates were giggling in the bathroom, admiring each other's dresses. She yelled out, "See you girls later!" as she passed. They got quiet for a moment and then wished her a good evening.

When Natalie went downstairs, Mrs. W. was reading the newspaper. Natalie saw her steal a glance from the side of the paper. "Lights out at eleven," Mrs. W. reminded her, just as Natalie's hand reached for the door.

She can't be serious, Natalie thought. She lit a cigarette and headed toward the bus stop. As Natalie waited for the bus, she considered her options. The truth was, she didn't have many. She resolved to stick around until she could save enough money to move to Las Vegas. She'd heard she could make money there as a waitress and by playing in pool tournaments. And she'd enjoy being in a city with a decent bar scene. She imagined herself gambling in the casinos and drinking in the nightclubs. For now, though, her local dive bar would have to do.

***

Over time, Natalie became friendly with her housemates, Sally and Miriam. Every week, the two girls would invite Natalie to their dance club. After declining for several weeks,

Natalie finally relented. Sally and Miriam were giddy with excitement as they helped each other zip dresses and fasten necklaces. Natalie felt like a fish out of water in her leather jacket and blue jeans.

The girls climbed into Sally's car. Alone in the back seat, Natalie lit a cigarette on the way to the dance hall. The girls looked at each other, then back at Natalie, when they heard her light up.

"You want to try one?" Natalie asked.

"Sure," they giggled nervously.

Natalie handed them the cigarette. Each girl took a short drag and then started coughing uncontrollably. Natalie chuckled and shook her head.

When the girls walked into the dance club, Natalie felt everyone staring at her. *How'd they get this many Howdy Doodies in one room?* Natalie wondered as the girls sat down.

"I'll grab us some Cokes," said Sally.

"Cokes? Where's the booze?" Natalie asked.

Miriam explained, "Oh, there's no alcohol allowed here. We have Coke, punch, or coffee."

No pool table, no bar! Just sing-song music and nerds dancing in their sweater vests. Natalie wondered why she'd said yes to this trip into Squaresville.

She went outside for a smoke. There were a few people already outside, cigarettes in hand. She lit her cigarette and said, "You guys come here often?"

They nodded, "Sometimes."

"Can't imagine why. There's no booze in this place!"

They laughed and opened their jackets to show Natalie their flasks. One of the guys handed his over so she could take a sip. She thanked him and went back inside for a bit, ducking out for smokes and swigs throughout the rest of the evening. As the girls drove home, Natalie decided the night hadn't been so bad. And she wondered where she could buy one of those flasks.

Time rolled on. Natalie went to work through the week and often played pool on the weekends. Once in a while, she'd tag along to the dance hall with her housemates. She still thought of them as silly, goodie-two-shoe types, but they got along alright.

Often, Natalie would sit by her bedroom window and light a cigarette. Before she could finish it, Mrs. W. would yell up, "You know there's no smoking in my house!" Natalie would roll her eyes, the other girls would giggle, and Natalie would put out her cigarette. She shared with the girls her plans to save up money and move to Las Vegas. She was getting close to being able to leave. Sally and Miriam seemed shocked, but they were interested in hearing more about Natalie's plans.

Sally and Miriam both wanted to find boyfriends and get married, have kids, and live happily ever after. Natalie would shake her head and laugh, "Girls, that's a fairy tale with a bad ending. Come to Vegas with me!" she'd tease. They'd giggle and wave their hands as if to say *no way!*

One Saturday night at the dance hall, an odd, skinny young man caught Natalie's attention. He seemed to be following Sally from a distance all evening. Occasionally, Sally would notice him standing nearby. He would say something to make her giggle. Natalie didn't like this guy. There was something about him that was just a little off. She stared at him hard, to let him know she was keeping an eye on him. He glared back in response.

Later, Natalie tried to caution Sally about the weirdo at the dance hall. But Sally insisted he was harmless, even sweet. "Besides," Sally protested, "I'm already twenty-two, and I can't afford to be too picky."

Sally and that creepy little guy from the club went on a few dates. His name was Fred, and he was a traveling salesman of some sort. One night, Sally and Fred were sitting outside on Mrs. W.'s porch swing, talking. Natalie couldn't hear their conversation, but she could hear Sally giggling from her window.

Natalie had just taken the second drag off her cigarette when Mrs. W. shouted up to her, "There's no smoking in my house!" So, Natalie headed downstairs to finish her smoke on the porch steps. Natalie nodded a hello to the couple in the porch swing. Sally giggled hello back, but Fred glared at her. He clearly didn't want Natalie intruding on their conversation. After a few minutes of awkward silence, Natalie stubbed out her cigarette and retreated to her room.

Sally went upstairs awhile later, dancing around like she had met Prince Charming.

"Sally, don't you think he's weird?" Natalie asked.

Sally looked like she had been slapped in the face.

Natalie continued, "C'mon, he still lives with his mother! He follows you around, even when you don't invite him. And he doesn't like any of us. I don't get a good sense from him, Sally."

"Oh, you are being silly, Natalie. I am going to marry him!" Sally announced.

"Did he propose to you?" Natalie asked, surprised.

"Well, not yet, but I know he will. He is taking me to meet his mother on Sunday."

"Yeah, that oughta be fun. Two weirdos!" Natalie scrunched her face in disgust.

Sally giggled and said, "Oh, Natalie, you don't like anybody! Goodnight."

Natalie had to admit, Sally wasn't totally wrong. Natalie didn't like most people. And she definitely did not like this creepy salesman, Fred. He set her nerves on edge. Her move to Las Vegas couldn't happen soon enough. She had already tacked up a wall calendar so she could mark down the days until she would leave Ford Heights for good …. seventy-nine days! Every day, she would mark off another square on the calendar.

Fred visited the boarding house often, so Sally must have gotten his mother's approval. Every Sunday, she would dress up in her best dress for dinner with Fred and his mother. When she would come home, she always went straight to bed. She never said much about the Sunday visits. Natalie found this behavior odd for a girl who usually wouldn't stop talking.

One day, Natalie decided to ask her how things were going with her boyfriend and future mother-in-law. Sally looked around before she answered, as if she didn't want anyone to hear her. She said, "Well, he really loves his mother. I am not sure she likes me very well."

"Sally, how could someone not like you? I don't like anybody, and you even wore me down!" Natalie teased.

Sally said, "I don't know. She always makes dinner for us. She and Fred talk throughout the meal. They never include me. Sometimes, I try to jump into the conversation. His mother will clear her throat and look at Fred. Then he shakes his head no to me."

"No? Like 'no talking,' no?" Natalie asked.

"I think so," Sally admitted.

"That's not good. That isn't how it should be. What's wrong with her? And what's wrong with him?" Natalie was confused.

"I'm not sure. After dinner, we watch TV together. There's no talking. He sits on the couch with his mother, and I sit in the chair. It feels … weird," Sally said.

"Did you ask him about it?"

"Yes," Sally looked down at her shoes. "He got angry with me and said to shut up."

"What? He told you to shut up? That's wrong! You need to break up with him. He is *not* the right guy for you." Natalie was furious. "Tell him to marry his damn mother, if that's how he feels."

Sally laughed, letting out a little snort. "Oh, Natalie. He just loves his mother, that's all. That's not wrong."

"It sounds like he loves her a little too much," Natalie cautioned. "You better straighten this situation out before you get married."

"I know!" she agreed.

The next day, when Natalie came home from work, Fred and Sally were standing on the front porch. It looked like they were arguing. Natalie saw Fred shove Sally and walk away. Natalie yelled at him, "Hey, don't shove her!"

He glared at her, then stormed off toward his car. Sally ran to her room, crying.

Natalie bounded upstairs to check on her friend. She knocked on the door and asked if Sally was okay. Sally cried harder but didn't open the door. Natalie turned to go to her room before Sally changed her mind about wanting to talk. Touchy-feely conversations weren't exactly Natalie's specialty. Sally opened the door, just as Natalie was making her retreat.

"He is so mad. He is so mad," she kept repeating.

"Why is he mad?" Natalie demanded.

"I told him what you said about his relationship with his mother wasn't right, and that I needed our relationship to change if we're going to get married one day. He is so mad, he is so mad. I don't think he'll ever come back," Sally cried.

"Sure, he will. He loves you, right?" Natalie tried to be comforting, but she was secretly relieved for her friend. Sally would be so much better off without this creep in her life. Still, Sally was crying into her pillow, heartbroken. Natalie tried a different approach. "There, there. You'll be okay. That's better ... Now, tell me what happened."

"Yes, well, I told him I thought it was a strange relationship he had with his mother. Weird. He got so mad, rageful. So, I got nervous and said, 'Natalie thinks so too.'" Sally said.

Oh, great, Natalie thought, *now you've dragged me into this. Thank God I am leaving in forty-seven days.* Natalie got up to change clothes and head out to the bar.

"You're leaving?" Sally looked hurt.

"Yes, Miriam will be home soon. She'll be more help than I am," Natalie said.

Natalie was leaving just as Miriam walked in the door. "She's all yours!" Natalie said to Miriam, motioning toward Sally.

Stepping off the porch, Natalie lit a cigarette and headed toward the bus stop. The sun had gone down, and the night was cold. She could see the lights from the bus stop, about a half a block away. She was just getting ready to quicken her pace to stave off the chill. She hesitated for a moment to check her jacket pocket for her flask. But her hand never made it to her pocket.

A heavy blow to the back of her head knocked her out cold. Fred shoved the hammer he was carrying into his waistband. He dragged Natalie to his car, pulled her into the back seat, and drove off toward home.

Once there, he looked around to make sure no one was watching. Fred pulled Natalie, still unconscious and bleeding, from his back seat and into his mother's backyard, where he had already dug a shallow grave. He slipped a rope around Natalie's neck and strangled her until he was sure she was dead. Satisfied with his work, he dumped Natalie's body into the hole near the canoe. Then he shoveled dirt on top of it.

Fred's mother, Alma, watched from the window until the last scoop of dirt had been placed. Once the curtain dropped, and the houselights were switched off, Fred took out his pocketknife. He carved the letter N on a rock and put it on top of Natalie's grave.

—Chapter 5—
Mrs. W.

I called and left another message for Officer Bradley.
Karen assured me she would pass along the name Natalie and
inquire again about the possibility of searching for the
makeshift cemetery on Alma's lot. I decided to search for
more answers. I sat quietly in my office with my eyes closed,
hoping to receive information about Polly from my sources on
the Other Side. Polly's was the next case I wanted to solve. I
was interested not just in the mystery of her death, but also the
story of her life. Who was she, and who did she hope to
become? Why was she so hard for me to reach?

In my mind's eye, a black-and-white scene appeared. The
scene was a kitchen, decorated in a mid-century fashion. A
shiny, chrome table and chairs stood out in the darkness. I
sensed someone sitting at the diner-style kitchen table. The
someone was a woman. I smelled cigarette smoke and heard

the soft sucking in of air, followed by a slow, purposeful exhale. A spiral of smoke floated on the darkness, up to the ceiling. The woman coughed, raspy and deep—a smoker's cough for sure.

I wasn't sure who should speak first. The silence was killing me. I whispered quietly, "Polly?"

The rhythm of the woman's smoking stopped, followed by more coughing.

No one answered, so I whispered again, "Polly, is that you?"

Still no answer. I stayed quiet. My attention was drawn to the window near the table, where I saw the faintest bit of movement outside. Someone was lurking in the shadows, watching and waiting.

"Oh, no!" I yelled aloud. Uncle Fred. My heart raced, and questions tumbled in my mind. *Who is he watching? Why is he here? Am I about to witness another murder from the past?* I held my breath and focused on the scene.

As my eyes adjusted to the dark kitchen, I could see the smoking woman was older and heavy-set. She wore an apron over her dress. Her hair was gray. Pink, foam curlers framed her face. She looked familiar. *Mrs. W.!* But why was my uncle watching her? And why was she smoking *inside the house*?

***

There was an empty lot across the alley from Mrs. W.'s house. Many nights, Fred would sit in the alley, watching who came and went from the boarding house. He was curious about which girls had fellas, and what hours everyone kept. Fred was calculating.

Mrs. W. noticed Fred wandering around near her house one day. She yelled out to him, "Get away from here, and don't come back. You know you're not allowed here!"

He yelled back, "I know that. You've made that perfectly clear to me, but I'd like to buy this lot across the alley from you. Do you know who owns the property?"

"What?" she snapped at him.

"I am buying a house near here, and I need to build myself a garage."

"Where?" she said, looking over her eyeglasses at him. "Where are you buying a house near here?"

Fred shouted out the address.

Mrs. W. rolled her eyes. "Well, I don't know anything about that lot," she shouted as she climbed her front porch steps. She looked back at him briefly and went inside, letting the screen door slam shut behind her.

Mrs. W. had reason to be suspicious of Fred. Three of the girls in her boarding house had dated him, then mysteriously disappeared. Their bodies had all been found in a nearby forest preserve. It was obvious to Mrs. W. that Fred had murdered these women. Why wasn't it obvious to the police?

That detective fellow had interviewed her several times. Once, he implied that she knew something. This made her furious, and she demanded he leave her home. She repeatedly told him he was looking in the wrong place.

"Go see that scrawny, little runt that lives across town with his mother," she told him. She never understood why Fred hadn't been arrested. He had to be a suspect. He was involved with those girls. She thought he was more than capable of murder.

Months after he'd first inquired about the property, Fred came back to see Mrs. W. This time, he knocked on her door. He carried a small stack of papers. When she answered the door, he shook the papers at her and said, "I've just been to city hall. This paperwork says you own that lot across the alley."

Mrs. W. was unimpressed. "It does, huh?"

"Yes, Mrs. W., it does!" He pointed toward the empty lot. "I would like to purchase this property to build a garage. How much would you sell it to me for?"

"You can't afford it," she said dismissively, shaking her head.

"Sure, I can. I can make you a full-price offer in cash. The tax records say it's worth $4,400."

"No, it's not. It's not for sale and certainly not for sale to you!" She slammed the door in his face.

Fred was frustrated. He did not understand her cold shoulder or disinterest in his offer. In Fred's mind, a full-price, cash offer was more than fair. He left, but he was seething.

Although he had said his plan was to build a garage, Fred had another motive for wanting the vacant lot. He had more things to hide. He needed a place that no one would suspect. The lot was ten miles or so from his mother's house and just a mile from a house he had been looking to buy in the neighborhood. Fred knew he needed to keep his trinkets out of sight, and this could be the perfect plan. Living with his mother had become complicated.

His mother was becoming more controlling and annoying with all her questions and her demands. One day he noticed her coming out of his attic bedroom. He was angry to find her near his stuff.

"What are you doing up there, Mother?" Fred demanded.

"I just wanted to see if it needed cleaning," she countered.

"Well, it doesn't," he spat. "Get out of there and don't ever come up here again."

She was furious and shocked that he talked to her that way. She swallowed her anger and stomped downstairs. Fred quickly checked the wall near his bed, where he had hidden his treasures. Keepsakes from each of his victims. Fred was relieved to see they were undisturbed. He heard his mother stomping in the kitchen. She slammed cupboards shut, muttering about what an ungrateful son she had raised.

When her clattering finally stopped, he crept downstairs and out the back door. He knew if he started the car, she would hear him. He opened the car door quietly and let the clutch out. He put the car in neutral and pushed it out onto the street and down the block. A few houses down, when he knew he was out of her earshot, he started the car and drove off.

He drove by Mrs. W.'s house. Circling the block a few times, Fred wondered when and how he could get his hands on her extra lot. He drove up and down the streets in the dark, looking at different houses in the neighborhood that might also work for his plan. He needed a place close to his mother's house and a quiet neighborhood for him to hide. Living close to his mother would keep her happy enough, and being close to the boarding house would suit him just fine.

Fred also wanted to keep an eye on Mrs. W. That old woman was a threat to him. She knew he had dated some of the girls who rented rooms from her. The same girls, in fact, who had been murdered. Fred felt that she had been watching him with a knowing glare. *She knows*, Fred told himself, *and no one can know.* He often wondered how he could get rid of her and make it look like an accident. But he hadn't yet concocted a plan that excited him.

Fred's interest in Mrs. W.'s property grew into a burning obsession. He drove by at different times of the day and night. Watching the house gave him a sense of purpose. He learned that he could conceal himself at a safe distance and gain a clear line of sight into her kitchen. He wanted that lot. He decided that he must have it, no matter the cost.

He wondered how he could get the old woman to change her mind about selling. He reasoned that he could afford to negotiate. He had a lucrative sales job, with a territory that spanned a three-hundred-mile radius from Ford Heights. Fred resolved to put his sales training to work for him as a buyer. Mrs. W. just needed a little convincing.

A year later, Fred was still driving by routinely. One day, as he watched Mrs. W. hang wet laundry on the clothesline, he noticed a sign in her window: *Two Rooms for Rent.* Fred was excited. He finally knew how he could persuade Mrs. W. to sell!

That evening, he knocked on the old woman's door. He knew she was home; there were lights on throughout the house. When she didn't answer, he knocked again—louder this time, almost pounding. After several moments, Mrs. W. finally answered the door. When she saw Fred standing on her front porch, her mood soured.

"What are you doing here? I told you to stay away!" she barked.

Fred slid into his most charming sales voice and said sweetly, "Well, Mrs. W., I am still interested in buying your empty lot. And from the looks of things"—he nodded to the vacancy sign—"it looks like you might need the money."

Mrs. W. wasn't interested in Fred being so close, but she did, in fact, need the money. After the string of murders, rumors circulated that Mrs. W. had been involved in the crimes. She was unable to rent out rooms in the years that followed. Her financial situation had deteriorated greatly.

She thought about how long Fred had been asking about her property. Maybe a little more waiting would work in her favor. If he was really set on buying the empty lot, who knew how much he might be willing to pay for it? Mrs. W. kept her face as cold as stone, betraying none of her calculations.

She pointed at the *Rooms for Rent* sign and snapped at him, "That's none of your business."

"I'm just trying to help both of us," he said, stepping forward.

"Stop!" she shouted, "I know you had something to do with those sweet girls' murders. You ... are a monster! There is no way I would ever do business with the likes of you. You need to leave, NOW!"

Fred abandoned all pretense in an instant. His eyes turned dark, and his mouth narrowed. Fred lunged at the old woman, just as she slammed the door in his face. Mrs. W. was not afraid of him. She knew how to protect herself. Although the money would help her, she wasn't willing to have a murderer for a neighbor. At least not right now.

—Chapter 6—
Detective Roman

Funny how a picture can be so calming, even when it is of someone you have never met in person. On one of my first visits to the Ford Heights police station, I snapped a cell-phone picture of Detective Roman's framed portrait in the hallway. I felt oddly close to him. He provided me with a sense of calm, and he had exceptional timing. He always showed up quietly in a corner whenever I needed him the most. From time to time, I would study his face in the picture. He looked smart and confident. There was a kindness about his presence, but a sadness in his eyes that haunted me.

I connected to Detective Roman's sorrow. I knew he died with the regret of never having found enough evidence to arrest my uncle. Every new murder case in the area served as a bitter reminder for Detective Roman of his failure. I could relate. I was feeling a similar level of frustration and futility.

I, too, had failed to make any real progress on the new Ford Heights cold cases. And my attempts to contact Bradley, to get him to help dig up the old missing-persons cases, were not yielding results either.

I lit some candles in my office before sitting down for my morning meditation practice. On my desk were the cold-case files I'd borrowed from Bradley. Next to those, I kept a notebook for jotting down bits of inspiration. There were three small, blue sticky notes on the cover of the notebook, one each for Teddy, Natalie, and Mrs. W. I'd also affixed a larger, yellow sticky note on the side of my computer monitor:

```
            Natalie
            Ruth
            Polly
            X?
         Cornfield?
```

I found myself struggling to connect the women in the folders to the women whose names I'd channeled. For that matter, I was struggling to make any new connections at all. I closed my eyes and began to repeat the women's names slowly, waiting for information to flow to me.

In an instant, I felt Detective Roman in the room. I was glad to feel him nearby. In my mind's eye, I could see him sitting in the corner of my office.

"Hi! I have missed you. I need your help now. I'm feeling stuck," I admitted. "What do I need to know now?"

He answered me with reassurance, "Lynn, trust that the information is coming."

"Can you help me?" I asked again.

"Of course," he replied. I felt him smile.

"So … Let's start with Polly. I've heard her name and felt her energy. She doesn't seem like a woman who would be Fred's type. I see her as a chain smoker, kind of rough-and-tumble. Does that seem right? Is that her?"

"You are sensing her right. She definitely wasn't Fred's type. For some reason, she liked him, and he found that interesting … at least for a while."

"For a while?"

"Their romance was short-lived. Once she met his mother, it was an instant no-go. His mother did not approve of such a promiscuous girl. His mother was not happy about their courtship," Detective Roman explained.

"Tell me more," I said with all the patience I could muster.

"Well, he met her at a park," Detective Roman said.

"A park? I can't imagine Fred going to a park!"

"He was sitting in the park near his home. He just needed time to think. He was trying to figure out what was next for him. He was overwhelmed with all that was going on. He felt very out of control. Fred had hoped to stop the killings, but the rage inside him had a strong pull. He felt so powerless most of the time. But when he held someone's life in his hands, he got to decide life or death. The power was intoxicating and all-consuming for him."

Detective Roman continued, "Oh, he never fooled me. I just could never prove he killed those women. Everything in me knew. My police instinct knew he was guilty. Unfortunately, the evidence was all circumstantial.

"In the early sixties, I heard about three women who had been found murdered in the Starved Rock area. Boy, it sounded just like Fred's MO. I even drove down there to meet with the local detectives and state investigators about the case. I couldn't pin that one on him either. He had one alibi after another."

"Wait," I interjected. "You're talking about the Starved Rock murders?"

"Yes, why?"

"I'm from that area. Remember, I grew up in Seneca. I had never heard about those murders until recently. A weird thing happened a few months ago. A copy of *Chicago Living Magazine* ended up in our driveway. It was all about those murders. At first, I thought maybe Fred was behind them, but some of my spirit guides set me straight."

"Well, you're welcome!" he chuckled.

"That was you?"

"Of course! Who do you think left you that magazine in the first place, Kid?"

Even though it was impossible for us to ever meet each other, I felt very close to Detective Roman. We had developed a kinship that I cannot explain.

"Why did you leave that for me?"

"Lynn, you needed some information about how murder investigations were performed in the 1960s. You also needed a few more pieces of the puzzle."

"The puzzle?"

"Yes, you are solving a puzzle. One that was thought to be unsolvable. I needed you to know that there are people out there who know things. Things they have never shared publicly. On their deathbeds, people tend to share their most private matters. So, stay vigilant. You will be getting a call. Don't brush it off. Take the call."

"Okay." I felt myself tense up.

"I am sending more people to help you. And that lab in Elgin will be of service to you soon. The lab in Elgin is a specialized forensic lab that can process contaminated DNA evidence to solve cold cases and other difficult crimes. They are the real deal," the detective said.

"Okay?" I was confused.

"Remember that, Lynn," Detective Roman cautioned.

I couldn't think of anything else to say. This wasn't what I expected to learn. I'd been hoping to hear stories from the victims. Instead, I received marching orders and technical instructions.

"Detective Roman, I am grateful for the help. I didn't realize the magazine was from you."

"Of course, Kid. I told you I would be with you until these cases are solved."

"Yes, yes, you did. And you have been, too. Most of the last five years have been overwhelming for me. Sometimes I doubt myself and feel like my imagination is getting the best of me."

"Well, stop that, Lynn. You don't have time for that. It never leads anywhere good. You were born to do this work, and these won't be your only cases. The universe needs you to keep helping many souls on the Other Side."

"I hope you will be by my side as I journey into this new line of work." *New line of work? Where in the world did that thought come from?* I wondered.

"Of course! Where am I going?" We both laughed.

True, I thought.

"I have more people for you to meet and help. Now, where exactly are you stuck?"

"Well, I keep hearing Polly's name and I know there's a woman named Ruth. At Fred's mother's house, Beth and I sensed four graves. Natalie also told me there are four graves there: P for Polly. N for Natalie, R for Ruth, and one marked X. But none of these women match the police files. It isn't adding up."

"It will. Trust me, it will."

"Okay. You know I do. Trust you, I mean," I stammered. "I have not been able to connect with Polly. I've tried several times, but she has not come through to me clearly. It seems strange. The first four women came through so quickly and easily. Teddy has told me about Polly, and Polly even visited me once but wouldn't speak. And I sometimes hear her name at night as I'm falling asleep. I just know there's something about her case that's going to be important."

"Lynn, you would be a good detective. You stay with the story, and you follow your instincts. That's important in police work."

I blushed and thanked him. I smiled because police work was never in my sights. "So, what happens next?"

"That depends. Are you ready?"

Am I ready? How can he ask me that? Of course, I am ready. Well ... am I? I shook my head to clear my self-doubt. Then I nodded.

"Yes! Yes, I am ready," I proclaimed.

"Here goes. X is a placeholder for a woman Fred tried to kill. She fought for her life and got away. She's still alive. Remember what the article confirmed? People know things and don't come forward. You will soon get a call from her son. She wants to help you," Detective Roman said.

"How does she know about me?" I asked. "Does she have the Gift as well?"

"No, nothing like that. She knows about the work you're doing. When she heard about your book, she asked her son to read it to her. She's quite old and unwell. The title with "Ford Heights" in it caught her attention. She has not told her son any of the details about this part of her life. She will ask him to find you."

Tensing up, I said, "Okay, I'm still listening."

"You must go see her in person. She will ask to meet with you and only you. It is important that you ask for permission to record her story. Be patient with her. It is hard for her to speak now. She will be leaving this world soon. She has carried this story for nearly sixty years. She never came forward. She was too scared to tell anyone. But what happened with Fred changed her whole life."

I felt the pang of empathy for this woman who'd held on to her traumatic secret for an entire lifetime. She'd been lucky, though, to have a lifetime beyond her dealings with my Uncle Fred. He had cut short the lifetimes of far too many women.

"Wait a minute!" I realized we'd made a mistake. "Why would Beth and Teddy say there were four bodies there? Why did we see four graves if this woman got away?"

"I can see why you felt it. Some of her belongings were buried in that spot. Fred's trinkets. You were probably picking up on that energy. Close your eyes. Now, what do you see?"

I followed his instructions. In my mind's eye, I saw a lavender sweater chain—like the ones women used to wear to fasten cardigan sweaters, a hair barrette, and a small book.

"Yes, Lynn, that's right. You are seeing it perfectly," Detective Roman said. "This woman and Fred struggled in his car for a few minutes. She got herself out of the car. He grabbed her by the throat and tried to choke her. He was pulling her into the backyard at his mother's house. During their struggle, her cardigan chain fell into the hole he had dug. She shoved him off her. He grabbed her hair as he stumbled. The barrette fell out of her hair.

81

"The only thing she could find to protect herself was a small hardback book she had in her purse. She threw it at him. It hit him in the head and knocked his glasses off. Fred fell into the hole he had dug for her. That gave her enough time to run away. She ran for her life. She managed to get a few blocks away before he climbed out of the hole and found his glasses. He drove up and down the road looking for her, hunting her. She was hiding behind someone's garage. She stayed there until she felt it was safe to find her way home.

"X was never the same after that. She was forever looking over her shoulder. Poor girl! I wish she had come to me. If only she had, maybe more women would have been saved," Detective Roman lamented. "I am not blaming her, mind you. She had to do what was right for her. X read the stories that followed in the newspapers. She never forgave herself for not speaking up about what happened to her. She wanted to do the right thing. She just couldn't find the courage to do it."

"How will I know it is her? What does X stand for?" I asked, my impatience creeping in.

"You will know, Lynn. You will know." Detective Roman let out a small sigh.

"Okay, I get it," I conceded.

"It is important for her to move on to heaven. She needs to unburden herself. She is a kind woman. You will like her.

Her son knows nothing of this story. He will be confused about why she insists on meeting you. But he'll call. He loves his mother and will honor her request. Do your part by taking the call," Detective Roman reminded me.

"Thank you for telling me. I will do exactly as you say," I promised. "When will I meet Polly and Ruth? Usually, souls come through very quickly to me when I call out to them."

"You will, Kid."

I thought, *if he says, "Wait for things to unfold" to me, I am going to scream. I am getting tired of hearing that phrase!*

"Okay. I won't say it, but that is the way it goes," Detective Roman answered.

I guess he knew what I was thinking.

—Chapter 7—
The Dead Woman's
Name Is Daisy

Sam and I had enjoyed a whirlwind of a weekend. Our niece's wedding meant entertaining out-of-town guests at our home for a few days. Between welcoming in family, shuffling them to the rehearsal dinner, attending the wedding and reception, and hosting a send-off Sunday brunch, we barely had time to sleep. Sam offered to take the last of our relatives to the airport on Monday morning so I could catch a much-needed nap.

Once I was alone, I closed my eyes and took a few deep breaths. Within a few moments, a familiar movie started playing again in my mind. I could sense someone running through a cornfield. The stalks were tall, dry, golden brown and brittle. Field corn, nearly ready for harvest. The spaces between the stalks formed a labyrinth, ripe for children's games. Just as I could see and feel the stalks, I could also smell the fall air.

I hear girls giggling. They are chasing each other through the rows of dried cornstalks. Three girls, maybe eleven or twelve years old, were enjoying the last throes of childhood before adolescence creeps in. They reach the end of the field and stop, out of breath from running. The girls all have broken pieces of corn husks on their clothes and in their hair. They see the mess they've made of themselves and fall on the ground laughing. Just as they begin to pick the husk pieces off their clothes, one of them scrunches up her nose.

"What stinks? Do you smell that? It's bad," she says, sniffing and looking around.

The other girls catch the scent. One holds her nose. The other says, "Phew, it must be coming from the water." She points to a small, murky pond close by. There are a few tall birds standing in the water near the edge of the pond.

The three girls walk towards the water. They're picking corn husks out of their hair, not watching their footing in the tall grass. The girl at the front of the pack, Evelyn, stumbles over something—a log, maybe. She falls to the ground. Pushing herself up from her belly, she twists around to see what caused her to trip. She screams hysterically. She sees a dead woman, half-clothed with a rope around her neck.

Evelyn scrambles up and away, and all three girls take off, as if running for their lives. One is screaming, "Oh, God! Oh, God! Oh, God!" The girls keep looking back, partially to make sure they're all still together and also to reassure themselves that they're gaining distance from what they've just seen.

They can see a house, and now so can I. They run towards it, yelling, "Nonna! Nonna!"

An older woman with dark, gray hair hangs her laundry on the clothesline behind the house. She sees the girls running towards her. She hears the panic in their voices and sees they are no longer playing their game of chase. Nonna yells to them in broken English, "Girls, what's a-going?"

"Nonna, Nonna. There's a woman. A woman." One of the girls is pointing back to the field.

Nonna is confused. "A woman, what you mean a woman? What are yous talking about? A woman?"

Gasping and hysterical, the youngest girl—Evelyn—says, "No, Nonna, not a woman. A woman's *body*." The young girl is trying to catch her breath.

Nonna eyes her with suspicion. The girls have played tricks on her before. "What do you mean, 'a woman.? 'A body'?" she asks them. "This is one of your games?"

An older girl hugs her, crying and shaking, "She's dead, Nonna. Out there, near the pond."

"Nonno!" The old woman yells for Evelyn's grandfather. "Come here! Come over here. These girls think they see something in the field. A woman, they say."

"What? Saw something?" He seems more interested than his wife. He walks over, more slowly than he'd like, legs stiff from years of farming. He looks like he has been working outside. He dabs his handkerchief on his forehead. "Now, what the devil is going on? What trouble did you girls get into?" he laughs, looking down at them.

"Nonno … it is real! We were running through the cornfield and went to sit by the pond. Evelyn tripped over a body. It's a woman, and we think she is dead," the girl named Millie says.

"Dead? What you do you mean, 'dead'?" He looks at them sternly.

"Dead like in the movies. Dead, Nonno." Evelyn says.

The other girls nod and say, "Dead."

"Well, c'mon now. Show me where." He seems skeptical.

The girls point toward the pond.

Nonno has already started walking into the field. He looks back at the girls, still standing near the clothesline. "I said, 'C'mon, girls!' Show me."

Nonno walks faster than normal, and the girls are reluctant to keep pace with him. When he notices them lagging behind him, he repeats, "C'mon, now. Show me."

About twenty yards from the body, the girls once again catch the odor of decay. They stop in their tracks. Evelyn points toward the pond while looking away, "She is there, Nonno."

The old man takes a few more steps forward before he picks up the horrible scent. He fishes a handkerchief out of his pocket to cover his nose and mouth. He bends down slowly. He inspects the small lump on the ground with obvious hesitation. He rolls the woman's body over until she is facing upward toward the sky.

He gasps and kneels next to her. "Oh, my. Oh, my Lord." Then he yells to the girls, "Run back to the house. Now! Tell Nonna to call the police. This poor young woman *is* dead!"

Evelyn and the other girls are in shock, finally believing what they saw with their own eyes. Their feet seem frozen in place. They don't move.

Nonno yells again, "Girls, NOW!"

His words somehow release them. They run back to Nonna, who has resumed hanging her wash in the backyard.

Evelyn runs the fastest. She crashes into Nonna's body, almost knocking her over and holding her tight. "Nonno said to call the police. She's dead! She's dead!"

Nonna takes a deep breath. She squeezes Evelyn for just a moment, then pries herself from Evelyn's grip. Nonna leads the girls to the porch and says, "You stay here. You no move."

The girls hear Nonna talking to the police on the phone. "We find a dead woman on our farm … Yes, I say 'dead.'"

Evelyn cannot hear the other end of the conversation, but she hears Nonna yell into the receiver, "Because my husband say she is dead!"

Nonna is upset and yelling in Italian. Evelyn doesn't recognize the words, but she knows the tone means trouble if Nonna doesn't see results. Evelyn is certain the police are on their way.

Nonno stays by the body until the police come. A county sherrif and two Illinois State Police cars finally pull up to the house. Nonna and the girls lead them out through the cornfield to where Nonno is waiting.

One of the policemen takes pictures. Another talks to Nonno, whose words tumble out quickly. A few times, he gestures back toward the girls. A few other policemen walk around the property. One lays a white sheet over the dead woman's body. Nonna makes the sign of the cross and looks toward the sky.

The sun will be setting soon. Nonna ushers the girls back toward the house. The girls' parents have all arrived. They listen to Nonna's recounting of the day's events and try to comfort their daughters. Nonna makes some iced tea, but no one is thirsty.

Another police car pulls up to the house, just as Nonno and some of the officers are making their way back. This car has different markings from the others.

"What's a city cop doing all the way out here?' one of the parents wonders.

The city cop steps out of his car. He shakes hands with the other officers, then with Nonno. Nonno and the city cop walk up the porch steps. Nonno motions for the girls to come over. Evelyn's wants to run away, but her legs freeze up again. The officer introduces himself as Detective Roman. "Detective Tom Roman," he repeats. He nods his head to the girls while holding onto his hat. Then he tucks his hat under his arm. He pulls a little notepad out from his coat pocket. "Can you girls tell me what happened?" he asks.

The girls look at each other, not knowing who should speak first. Millie nudges Evelyn with her elbow. Evelyn clears her throat and replays for him what happened. As she finishes her story, she starts crying.

Nonna steps in and lovingly puts her arms around Evelyn, pulling her close. Nonna glares at Detective Roman and says, "That's enough, for now. Sir, she is young girl. This is too much for young girl."

Detective Roman hesitates. He has more questions, but he can see Evelyn's distress. Satisfied he has what he needs for now, he nods and closes his notepad. He walks around back and heads through the field to see the dead girl for himself.

Detective Roman uncovers the dead body and kneels to look at her. When he notices the rope around her neck, he gets a sinking feeling.

Daisy! This dead woman's name is Daisy. She sang Friday and Saturday nights in a nearby nightclub. Her mother reported her missing a few days ago. Her roommate thought she may have left town to follow a dream of singing in Hollywood.

Detective Roman frowns. *Strangled, half-naked, all too familiar. Could this murder be related to his Ford Heights cases from the late fifties? Or something entirely new?* The detective suspects he'll find a connection between this girl and a certain scrawny, little creep back in Ford Heights.

The county coroner's black car has arrived, pulling off a country road nearer to the crime scene than to the farmhouse. A stocky man makes his way to Detective Roman. They talk a bit but look more at the body on the ground than at one another. The coroner waves in his men, who approach with a stretcher. They nod to the detective, load up the woman's body, and carry it back to the waiting vehicle. The coroner and his men close the doors and pull slowly out onto the country road.

The policemen walk the area, scouring the grass around the pond and the cornfield for clues. Out of the corner of his eye, Detective Roman spies a scrap of white paper in the grass. He bends to pick it up. He notices the card is ripped in half, and the ink on it is smeared and faded, washed out from moisture and sunlight. He can make out what looks like part of a phone number and a pink business logo. He slips the paper into a plastic bag and then into his coat pocket, hoping the state cops didn't notice. He promises himself he will check this into evidence later. But first, he wants to visit some flower shops in Ford Heights.

***

I opened my eyes and grabbed my notebook. I began writing so quickly that I wondered whether I'd be able to read the notes later. Still, I felt a sense of urgency to capture everything, just as I had seen it. I knew this vision held the key to more than just Daisy's murder.

Rereading my notes, I gave a knowing smirk at the thought of Detective Roman rolling up on a remote, country crime scene just to see if he could pin the crime on my Uncle Fred. *Wait!* I suddenly realized that Daisy wasn't found in Ford Heights at all. I grabbed my phone and rang Karen at the Ford Heights Police Department.

"Hey, Karen! It's Lynn Monroe," I chimed.

"Oh, hey, Lynn. He's not—" she started.

"No, I know. Bradley's 'not available.' I'm actually wondering if *you* can help me," I said.

"Oh? What exactly do you need?" asked Karen. I liked her conspiratorial tone.

"Well … I have a hunch about a case, but it's not one of Bradley's. Who has jurisdiction for cases out in rural areas?" I asked.

"Could be county, could be state. Just depends on the nature of the crime. What else can you tell me?"

After a little more discussion, Karen said that it shouldn't be a problem for her office to get copies of investigative records from the state police archives.

"In that case," I said, "I'd like to make an appointment with Bradley to review the state's cold-case file on Daisy Larson."

"I'll make sure both he and the file are available next Tuesday," Karen assured me. "Can you be here around lunchtime?"

"Yes, and I'll bring lunch!" I said, my mood suddenly lifted.

—Chapter 8—
Daisy's Demise

The following Tuesday, I parked in front of the Ford Heights Police Department and stepped out with a renewed sense of purpose. I texted Karen and waited by my open trunk. She came out with a small trolley to help me cart in several large gourmet sandwich platters, gallons of tea and lemonade, and cookie trays. Apparently, when word got out that someone was bringing in lunch, lots of people suddenly found office work to attend to on Tuesday.

I didn't mind. I was grateful to the entire police department for their service. And I hoped it would help me win over Officer Bradley. I'd heard a rumor that he couldn't resist a good butter cookie.

Bradley spotted me as Karen and I were setting up the lunch spread. I saw him register a look of surprise, then one of amusement. He realized he'd been hoodwinked, but he seemed to be a good sport about it. He walked over to me.

"Okay, Lynn. You got me," he admitted. "What do you need?"

"I'm so glad I caught you while you at the station!" I said. My tone was cheerfully ironic. "Maybe, after lunch, you and I can talk about the cold case involving Daisy Larson? I'd like a chance to connect to it and see where it leads me. Our favorite 'old detective' seemed quite interested in the case."

"Well, that all depends," Bradley hesitated. "Are there cookies?"

"Yes! In fact, I've just come from a bakery where they sell the most delicious cafeteria-style butter cookies in all of Chicago."

"Aha! Karen!" Bradley had found his suspect. He realized he was smiling and quickly hardened his expression. "I've been wondering how that file ended up on my desk. Yes, that old detective fingered your uncle for the murder, but he couldn't produce enough evidence to get the state to take him seriously."

He continued, "I can give you ten minutes after lunch. I really can't be wast—spending too much time on these unsolvable cases, Lynn. Don't take it personally. But I have real police work to do."

"Understood." His words stung, but I was willing to take any opening I could get.

Once the sandwich and cookie platters had been decimated, I tracked Bradley down at his desk. As promised, he handed me a thick accordion file with all the notes from Daisy's case. "Printed from digital archives," he explained.

I asked him if I could sit alone with the file in one of the "fishbowls," the small, glass-enclosed meeting rooms that reminded me of old phone booths.

"Yeah, no problem," he was clearly relieved that I wasn't asking for his help.

I carried the folder into one of the fishbowls, feeling a little self-conscious. Usually when I do my spiritual work, it's not on display for everyone to see. Still, I had a job to do. I skimmed the pages of the file. A black-and-white photocopy caught my eye: the visible outline of a torn scrap of paper with a smudge in one corner. Closer inspection revealed a faded, partial phone number. The smudge might have been a rose or a tulip at one point. *Daisy's flower card!*

I set all the papers preceding this one in a face-down stack on the left side of the small table, careful to preserve the ordering of the file. The remaining stack of papers I placed face-up to the right. The image of the flower card stared up at me. I placed my hands on it to connect my energy to it. Then I closed my eyes and slowed my breathing.

***

Daisy grew up in the quiet, suburban town of Crete, Illinois, with two parents, several siblings, a dog, and a grandmother. Daisy was named for her mother's favorite flower. She was an average student but aspired to fame and fortune. She did not want to be a nurse, a schoolteacher, or—heaven forbid!—a secretary. She wanted to be a famous singer and actress like her idol, Marilyn Monroe. Daisy, too, was a shapely girl in her early twenties. She had dreamy, blue eyes and bleach-blonde, teased hair. Although she was a natural blonde, she stripped her hair a few shades lighter to look more like Marilyn's.

After high school, Daisy worked as a clerk at the local grocery store during the week and lived with her cousin, Alice, to save money. Everyone agreed that Daisy had the voice of an angel when she sang in the church choir on Sundays.

But her weekend nightclub act was flirty and suggestive. She loved interacting with the audience and craved the male attention. She had a regular following at the club. The regulars loved to hear her sing. She was funny and told bawdy jokes between songs. She sang so sweetly in the choir and so seductively in the night club. It was hard to believe it was the same person singing.

Daisy's personality was more like her nightclub persona than that of a church choir songbird. She liked getting drunk and having a good time. She loved sipping scotch. Scotch was a man's drink in those days, but Daisy didn't care—she loved the smell and taste of it.

Daisy had her own car, a 1956 Caribbean-turquoise Ford Fairlane convertible. The turquoise color was striking, and the white-wall tires made her car stand out. Daisy's cousin Alice and their friends were all impressed by Daisy's bold style and her unapologetic ambition to become famous. They admired Daisy's stage clothes, her fancy car, the way she sipped her scotch, smoked her long cigarettes in between sets and signed the occasional autograph.

In truth, Daisy fantasized about moving to Hollywood someday. The pay was good, she'd heard, and if she played her cards right, one of those Hollywood agents could make her a big star. The marquee of every movie house in America would say *Daisy!* She dreamed of seeing her name in lights.

The money at the club was decent for a part-time gig. The manager would tell her to forget Hollywood. "You have a great career here, Daisy," he'd tease.

She would laugh it off. "Here? No, not here. I am only here until I have enough money to move to Hollywood and see my name in lights. '*Daisy!*'" When said her name, she sang it with an upward trill and waved her hand in a flourish.

Daisy's parents didn't approve of her lifestyle. They loved Daisy and appreciated that she made it home for holidays and family birthdays. Sometimes she even joined them for Sunday dinner after church.

Daisy had learned to sing in the church and barely missed a service growing up. Everyone loved her at church, except Mrs. Radcliff. She felt Daisy's lifestyle was inappropriate and set a bad example in the congregation. In the pews, Mrs. Radcliff and her lady friends openly complained about Daisy and her "wilding" ways. This never bothered Daisy. It did, however, hurt Daisy's parents. Discussions at home usually ended at an impasse, but never in an argument.

Back at her weekday job as a grocery clerk, Daisy got a kick out of flirting with the single men who shopped there. She had many admirers, many of whom dreamed of marrying her. She had a way of making them think she only had eyes for them. Except that wasn't true; she had eyes for *all* of them. She had been in love before. But it never lasted. Most of her suitors wanted her to marry her and have her raise a household of kids. That life was not for her!

Every Tuesday morning, a seemingly quiet, well-dressed man would come in to buy groceries with his mother. He was quite smitten with Daisy. Every time he got near Daisy, this man would turn into a nervous little boy. Daisy thought it was sweet to see a grown man behave this way around her. She could make him blush easily. "Freddy, how arrrrrre you?" she would giggle with a teasing voice. His mother would become visibly agitated if he talked too long with Daisy.

"Let's go!" she would order him, snapping her purse shut. If he hesitated, she would raise her voice and say, "I said *now*, Fred."

He would shrug his shoulders and say, "Well, I guess I have to go. See you next time, Daisy." He would sing her name, like in the song about the bicycle built for two. Then he would smile shyly and walk away, looking for all the world like a man in love.

His mother didn't disguise her irritation. She would say, "You are making a fool of yourself, Fred. She's nothing but a floozy."

One day, Daisy noticed Fred in the store by himself. She saw him in the distance and gave him a big, Daisy-hello wave. She didn't think he saw her, so she yelled out, "Freddy, are you lost? It's Thursday." He looked at her but did not acknowledge her excited greeting.

This happened every now and then. He would come in on a Thursday, she would shout hello to him, and he would not acknowledge her. He never checked out in her lane on Thursdays. She wondered what he was doing there on a different day because he was such a regular Tuesday shopper.

One Thursday, she decided she didn't like being ignored by Fred. Feeling a little bold, she yelled out, "Hey, Fred, come and check out with me today."

He looked uncomfortable but said, "Okay, I will." He moved over to her check-out lane and set a half-gallon of orange juice on the counter. Daisy rang up the juice and said in her sexy, nightclub voice, "That's it? Just orange juice?" She tilted her head slightly to the right.

Fred looked down, seemingly embarrassed, and said, "Yes, we forgot this on Tuesday."

She joked, "Well, I forget things all the time!" She was teasing him, and he willingly took the bait. They bantered back-and-forth for a few moments.

An older woman was waiting impatiently behind Fred. She cleared her throat and said in a sternly to Daisy, "Can you check me out, please?" She was clearly annoyed, not just by being delayed, but also by their brazen flirting. She glared at Daisy and Fred disapprovingly. The two young people exchanged knowing glances and laughed. Fred left the checkout lane quickly.

Fred continued to shop weekly with his mother on Tuesdays. Daisy noticed him making an extra trip to the store every Thursday. He always had the same story about forgetting something. Daisy liked teasing him. He was shy and sweet, different from most of the men she met. She was starting to like him.

Daisy told her cousin Alice about Fred. She confided in Alice that she was going to invite him to come and see her sing at the club. Alice said, "Are you sure you should do that? Daisy, you have plenty of boyfriends and admirers. Why do you need another one?"

"This guy's different," Daisy countered.

Alice continued, "He sure sounds 'different.' Maybe you should leave him alone. He doesn't sound like your type. He's quiet and shy. And he lives with his mother? C'mon!"

Daisy thought Alice sounded jealous. So she laughed it off and said, "I know what I'm doing."

The truth was, Daisy did have her pick of men. She would date them, get bored quickly and break up with them. Over and over, the same routine. Daisy's brokenhearted callers would come crying to Alice, wanting to know what had happened with Daisy. They would beg Alice to get them a second chance to date Daisy.

Alice wanted to say to them, *What do you mean, 'What happened?' Daisy's a floozy who used you for a nice dinner and drinks! How can you be so stupid?* But she would bite her tongue and say instead, "I don't know. I'm sorry things didn't work out. I'll tell Daisy you came by to see her."

The next Thursday, Daisy saw Fred come into the store. This time he had a bag of apples. She said, "Oh, Fred, what are you going to do with a whole bag of apples? Make me a pie?"

He stuttered and stammered. "Oh, my mother needs these. I forget what for. She just needs them."

"You know, Freddy," she lowered her body and leaned towards him, "you've been forgetting something every week now. I think you just like come to see me." She smiled at him with her pink, pouty lips and dreamy blue eyes.

Fred was clearly ruffled. "No! It's not like that." He paid for his apples and almost ran toward the door.

Daisy laughed and said out loud to the bagboy, "Oh, boy!"

The bagboy said, "I think you scared this one off, Daisy!"

She threw back her head in raucous laughter. "Oh, well," she said, but secretly wondered if she had let one get away.

She did scare Fred off. He stayed away on Thursdays for several weeks. On Tuesdays, he barely talked to her. In fact, he started going to another check-out lane on Tuesdays.

Daisy wondered what had happened, why Fred was suddenly avoiding her. She decided to find out. The next time she saw him leaving the store, she called out to him loudly, "Goodbye, Freddy!"

Fred jumped. He seemed startled and kept his head down, almost running towards the exit. When he got to the exit door, he turned back and smiled sweetly at Daisy.

The next Thursday, Fred was back. He came to Daisy's checkout lane with a loaf of sliced wheat bread.

He grinned and said shyly, "Hi, Daisy."

"Well, hello, Stranger! I guess you're better at remembering all your groceries now. I've missed seeing you." She twisted her body a little, flirting with her dreamy blue eyes.

"Oh, yeah. Yeah. We haven't forgotten anything lately, I guess." he stammered.

"Did you know that on the weekends I sing at a nightclub across town?" Daisy continued.

"Oh. You're a singer?" Fred seemed curious.

"Yes, I love singing. You should come by some time. What's your favorite song? I'll sing it to you." She smiled and touched his hand lightly as she took his money for the bread.

He snatched his hand away and said, "I don't have a favorite song." Then he snapped at her, "Can I have my change? I need to get going. Mother is waiting."

Surprised by his curtness, Daisy said, "Here you go." She leaned in and handed him his change slowly. This time he did run out.

The bagboy said, "Geez, Daisy!"

"Oh, it's harmless. I'm just having some fun!" she joked.

That Saturday evening, Daisy was back on stage singing and dancing, feeling alive and free. After her first set, she returned to her dressing room to take a short break. She was surprised to see a vase of red roses had been delivered for her. She opened the card. It read:

My favorite song is
"I Wanna Be Loved by You."
Your Admirer, Freddy.

Daisy giggled to herself. When Daisy took the stage for her second set, she searched the audience for Fred. No Freddy. Disappointed, she sang the song anyway. Before she started singing, she announced, "I have a song requested by my friend, Freddy." She sang it in perfect Marilyn Monroe fashion.

Fred wasn't in the audience; he was listening from the nightclub entryway. He loved Daisy's voice and loved hearing his name come off her lips even more. He vowed to himself that he would return.

Every Saturday evening that summer, Daisy would find a fresh vase of red roses in her dressing room. There would always be a note from Freddy requesting his favorite song. Daisy would sing it every week. Fred stayed out of sight in the entryway. This was safer for him.

The weekly rose delivery and song routine continued into the fall. After her final set one night, Daisy was tired and decided to head straight home instead of winding down in her dressing room. She stepped out the back door of the nightclub. When the chilly fall air hit her bare arms, she remembered she had forgotten her coat inside. Shivering from the cold, she went back inside to get her coat. She didn't notice Fred in the parking lot. He was waiting there, planning to watch her walk to her car like he had been doing for a long time now.

While Daisy was inside, Fred walked up to her car and lifted the passenger side door handle. The door was unlocked, so he got into the passenger seat. Moments later, Daisy got in and started the car. She jumped when she saw him in the front passenger seat. "Oh, hi, Freddy! You scared me! What are you doing here?" She caught her breath and asked, "Were you in the audience tonight? I didn't see you."

"Well, you knew I was there. You got my flowers, and I heard you sing to me." As he moved toward her, his voice was different. Low and creepy. She had not heard him talk like that before, and it was unsettling.

She yelled, "Fred. Stop!" She raised her hand and pushed hm away. "Stop!" she shouted louder.

The bartender was walking to his car and heard Daisy yelling. He walked up to her car.

Looking in, he said, "Hey, is everything okay here?" As he leaned down into the car window, he saw a man in the front seat. "Daisy, is this guy bothering you?"

Daisy was nervous and definitely startled. She said, "No, he's an old friend." She moved closer to the window. She tried to make eye contact with the bartender and signal to him she was scared. Still, she was afraid of saying anything that might make Fred more aggressive.

Fred got spooked by the bartender's interruption. Knowing he'd overstayed his welcome, he clamored out of Daisy's car. He walked to his car with haste, squealing his tires as he drove away.

Concerned, the bartender asked, "What was that all about, Daisy?"

"Oh, just a fan. I'm good." Her hands were trembling as she tried to light her cigarette.

Seeing this, the bartender said, "I'll follow you home." Daisy nodded in agreement.

Daisy was still shaken when she got home. She locked the doors and double-checked them all. Why would Fred scare her like that? She could sense another side to shy Freddy that she hadn't expected and didn't like. She tossed and turned, trying to shake the feeling that she was being watched. She even considered waking Alice up. She knew Alice would just say, "I told you so." *This time,* she thought, *Alice is probably right.*

Daisy decided she would no longer accept Freddy's flowers nor sing his favorite song in the club. What she had chalked up to a "sweet, harmless crush" now seemed dangerous. She felt violated. She wasn't sure what to do. She could report what happened, but what had happened really? And to whom would she even report it? She wondered if she should stop being nice to Fred. Confront him? Quit her job? She decided she was overreacting. *Best to just ignore the problem and let it go away on its own*, she concluded.

She still saw Fred and his mother at the grocery store on Tuesdays. He stopped coming in on Thursdays. The flowers stopped on Saturdays. She felt relieved and told herself that he had probably moved on. She hoped he really had.

For nearly a year, she didn't give the situation more than a passing thought. But one night the following September, Daisy walked into her dressing room to find a vase of red roses with a familiar note. She panicked, shivers running up her spine.

She grabbed the stage manager by his shirt collar and said, "Where did these flowers come from? Who brought these? I can't go back on stage." She was starting to hyperventilate.

The manager was confused by her actions. He said, "You okay? You are acting weird. Daisy, we have fifty people out there that have paid there hear you sing. You've got to sing."

"Take these flowers out of here! Throw them out. Now!" She shouted, her voice trembling.

"Okay, okay," he said, muttering "crazy broad" under his breath. He took the flowers outside and tossed them into a dumpster in the alleyway.

Fred was sitting in his car, waiting for Daisy to leave for the night. He hadn't gone into the club at all, not wanting to be seen. He watched, horrified, at Daisy's flowers—*his* flowers—being discarded like garbage. He ran to the dumpster and retrieved them. He tugged at the note card that had been attached to the vase. He ripped the card in half, then pocketed the pieces like a pouting schoolboy.

Then he saw Daisy's car parked in the lot next to the building. *So she is here!* He threw the roses back in the garbage and walked over to Daisy's car. The door was unlocked again. He slipped into her backseat to wait for her.

"How can she throw my flowers away? How can she throw my love away?" he wondered. He waited for a few hours, shivering in the autumn cold. Finally, he heard cars start up nearby and drive away. He looked up from the backseat to see the parking lot was nearly empty. *Just a few cars left*, he thought to himself.

He heard the nightclub's backdoor open and shut. Then he heard Daisy's sweet voice saying goodnight to someone. Fred lay low in her backseat. He needed to be sure she was alone. He heard a man say, "Should I follow you home?" Fred recognized the voice of the bartender who had stopped him from making his move with Daisy.

"NO!" Daisy laughed, "I'm okay. See you next weekend. Thank you, though. You are a doll!" She blew him a kiss as she got into her car.

Fred watched while Daisy started the car. Daisy turned on the heater and fiddled with the radio. Then she noticed her bartender friend approaching the car. She rolled down her window and waved for him to go. "Bye! I am fine. Really, I am." Daisy pulled out onto the street and headed toward home.

About a mile down the road, Fred sat up in the backseat and said, "Hello, Daisy. I've missed you."

Daisy gasped and nearly swerved off the road. Her heart leapt into her throat. She wanted to scream, but no sound was coming out. She knew no one would hear her anyways. She put both of her hands together on the wheel. Looking in her rear-view mirror, she said to Fred, "What are you doing here, Fred?" She tried to sound tough.

"Don't you mean 'Freddy'?" he teased.

"What are you doing here, *Fred*?" she repeated, more firmly.

From the backseat, Fred slipped a length of rope around Daisy's slender neck and pulled her body back towards him. She gasped for air. His voice was low and angry. "You're going to sing for me now, Daisy. Aren't you?"

"No!" she choked, shaking her head back and forth to free herself. She tried grabbing the rope with one hand to loosen it from around her neck. She was losing control of her car, and it began to swerve. Daisy's mind raced. She decided that if she could crash the car, she might have a chance to get away.

Fred pulled the rope tighter and shouted, "Drive, Daisy, drive! Turn here. I said, turn here!"

Daisy couldn't make sense of his words and could barely see the road in front of her. She was trying to breathe and plan her escape. She felt like she could die any minute at the hands of a madman. *Why had I not listened to Alice? Why? She told me. She told me to stay away.*

Fred kept the rope tight enough around her neck to keep her under his control, but not so tight that she would lose consciousness. He had developed a feel for the right amount of pressure. And he needed her to drive out of town.

Daisy realized they were now on a dark country road. She had not been paying attention to how they got there. She had no idea where they were. She tried to tell him to stop, but the rope was too tight for her words to come out. Fred held the rope tight and muttered under his breath about how ungrateful she had been.

"Sing my song, Daisy," he demanded.

She tried to sing, hoping it might distract him. Appease him. Anything. She struggled to get the words out, "Loosen… loosen the rope…," she choked, "so I can sing for you."

He hesitated but did loosen his grip on the rope. Daisy started singing, "I Wanna Be Loved by You." She choked back tears, but she kept singing. She could feel the rope loosen a little more from around her neck.

She saw a bridge ahead in the darkness. She knew her only chance of survival was to crash the car and run away. She kept singing. She closed her eyes and stomped on the gas pedal. When she accelerated, Fred fell back into the backseat.

"What are you doing?" he spat before realization set in. Then the car crashed head-on into the bridge.

Daisy's head hit the steering wheel, knocking her unconscious. Fred was shaken from the crash, and furious with Daisy besides. He climbed into the front seat and shoved her over. He had to get the car back on the road before someone drove by. Before he put the car in drive, he grabbed his rope and strangled Daisy until he was sure she was dead. He kept driving further out into the country, frantically looking for a place to dump her body. He was yelling at her, "Should have sung my song, Daisy. Should have sung my song." His anger intensified into an all-consuming rage.

Fred saw light from a farmhouse in the distance. He turned onto a dirt road and drove roughly in the direction of the house. He wasn't sure where he was, but the surrounding cornfields would provide enough cover for what he had to do next.

He pulled the car off the road—far enough away from the house to avoid being noticed—and drove a few feet into the field. He put the car in park and looked over at Daisy, her body slumped over in the passenger seat. He shook her and sobbed, "My sweet Daisy. Why didn't you sing for me? Daisy, I love you! I love you! Why didn't you sing to me? Why didn't you sing to me?"

His sadness gave way again to anger. It didn't have to be this way! She shouldn't have refused his flowers, shouldn't have thrown away his affection for her. This was all her fault, and he hadn't finished making her pay for what she'd done. He became excited, knowing she was now completely under his control. He grabbed her then and began kissing her as he removed her blouse. He hadn't felt this free with a woman in years, and there was nothing she could do now to stop him. And he didn't stop until his rage and lust subsided.

His eyes had adjusted to the night. He could see a pond just ahead. He slung Daisy's lifeless body over his shoulder and dumped her in the tall grass near the water. He shoved his hands in his pockets to stave off the cold as he said his last goodbye. A moment later, he wiped his nose with his sleeve. He didn't notice a part of his flower card fall out of his pocket onto the grass. He ran back to Daisy's car and drove back into town. He pulled her car into the nightclub parking lot and parked it back into her original spot.

Fred knew the front of her car was damaged, but it was drivable. He took his handkerchief and wiped the front and back seats along with the steering wheel. When he was done, he ran to his car, which he had parked across the street. Driving home, he could hear her voice. She was singing his song. He couldn't get the singing out of his head. He drove home to his mother's house and went right upstairs to his room.

Fred tossed and turned all night. He could not sleep. The evening had gone so wrong. *How did this happen again?* he wondered.

***

"I'll take that ten minutes now," I said to Bradley, handing him the file. I was still wiping the tears from my eyes.

He looked uneasy. "A deal's a deal," he said.

"My uncle killed this girl, and I know how we can prove it," I asserted.

"I'm listening," Bradley said. He looked skeptical.

"There's a forensics lab in Elgin. They can process contaminated evidence from old crime scenes and extract DNA, right?" I waited for Bradley's nod. "My uncle's DNA was a match to the cases we solved before, so I know you've got a record of it. Can you have the state police see if he's a match for this case, too?"

Bradley thought for a moment. I could see his mental gears turning. "I'll see what I can do, Lynn. In fact, I'll see if Captain Simon can help. Surely someone over there owes him a favor."

"Great! I have eight minutes left, by my calculations," I'd found my opening.

Bradley slumped a little in his chair. "Okay. What else?"

"Do missing-persons cases ever expire?" I asked.

"No, they're either solved when the person is found, or they stay open indefinitely. Doesn't mean anyone is actually looking for them, though. We don't spend a lot of time on them. Too many dead ends. Takes up valuable resources." He raised his eyebrows at me and pursed his lips.

"I get that. I do. It's just, if the bodies were never found, then the cases would still be open, right? They still exist somewhere … if someone did have the resources to find them?" I asked.

"In theory," Bradley was closing up again.

"And under what circumstances might those resources become available?" I probed, adding, "In theory?"

"If we find a John Doe—or in this case, a Jane Doe, we try to match it against missing persons before we close the case," he said. "We would need hard evidence, Lynn. Not just a hunch or a vision or whatever your uncle might have told you before he died."

"I get where you're coming from," I said. This guy was humoring me, but he thought I was a total quack. I took a deep breath and pressed on. "You'll let me know if he's a match for Daisy, though, right? She's not a missing person. They found her out in the country."

"Yes, I'll see what we can do about Daisy. And I'll have Karen call you if we learn anything." I was being dismissed.

I tilted my head toward the clock on the wall. "Looks like I've used my ten minutes. Thank you, Officer Bradley."

"Just Bradley."

"Thank you, Bradley." I laid a small box of butter cookies on Bradley's desk and turned toward the front door.

On my way out, Karen gave me a quizzical look. I shot her back a quick wink. We were making progress.

—Chapter 9—
R is for Ruth

R is for Ruth. R is for Ruth. R is for Ruth. I kept repeating that phrase with the hope that it would bring her forward. Who was Ruth? She didn't seem to want to talk to me. Or maybe it wasn't time for us to talk. I was confused and discouraged. Despite my success with Daisy, I began to wonder if I was as proficient with my medium gift as I'd thought. After all, I had been trying for a long time to connect with Ruth and Polly.

Feeling a bit defeated, I sat quietly at my desk with my eyes closed. In my mind, an image of a room appeared. The room was filled with containers of flowers. So many flowers! I saw roses, tulips, daffodils, snapdragons, carnations, large bunches of baby's breath, and lots of greenery.

I kept my eyes closed and looked around the room. It was a small space with pale yellow walls and bright, white-trimmed woodwork. At the front of the room, I saw an old, brass cash register atop a dark, wooden counter. Behind the counter was a large roll of white butcher paper, boxes of colored tissue paper, and spools of ribbon in all different colors.

I was suddenly awash in the smell of fresh flowers. I felt like I had just walked into Phillips, my favorite local flower store. I inhaled deeply and let my senses take over. *Why am I in a flower shop?*

Then I saw a petite, young woman with a dance in her step. She reminded me of prim-and-proper Sandy from the movie *Grease*. She emerged from the stockroom carrying a huge bouquet of orange tiger lilies. She carefully laid them on the counter, bending down to smell them as she did so. I saw her tear off a large piece of the white butcher paper. She moved the lilies onto the paper and wrapped the paper around them in a cone shape. She slid over to the collection of ribbons, where she paused and tilted her head to one side. She seemed to be contemplating the perfect color of ribbon for this bouquet. After a few moments, she pulled out a spool of thick, purple ribbon. She cut a long piece from the spool and tied it around the bouquet into a perfect bow.

She held the bouquet up and smiled to herself, seeming satisfied with her creation. I heard a bell and the sound of a door opening. The girl looked up toward the door and smiled.

"Well, hello, Mr. Johnson! You have perfect timing. I just finished your wife's bouquet." Proud of her work, she lifted the bouquet for his approval. "That will be $6.25."

The man reached into his wallet and handed her the money. The young woman punched the sales amount into the cash register, and the money drawer opened with a *ka-ching!* sound. She counted back his change.

As he put the change in his pocket, he said, "Thank you, Ruth. I know my wife will love these flowers."

Ruth! Oh, my God, it's Ruth! I'm finally connecting with Ruth! I had to calm my breathing again. Just as I was about to introduce myself to her, I heard the door open again.

Ruth greeted him with a warm welcome. "Hi, Fred! How are you doing today?"

My uncle. I kept watching.

"I need some flowers. Roses. You know, red ones."

"I sure do, Fred. That is some lucky girl, getting roses from you every Saturday."

I could see Fred was uncomfortable and trying not to talk too much. He almost seemed nervous. "Yes, she's lucky. Very lucky. I am running late. Will this take long?" He shifted his weight from foot to foot. His hands were thrust deep in his pants pockets.

"I will have them ready for you in no time! Give me a few minutes. Are we doing paper or a vase this week?"

"Paper," he grunted at her. While he was waiting, he walked around the store looking at the flowers. From time to time, he looked down at his watch.

Ruth was humming to herself as she arranged the roses on the counter. "How do you like these, Fred?"

He barely looked at them and muttered, "They are fine, just fine. Will it be much longer?"

She joked, "Oh, Fred, you are always in a hurry. Every week, you are in a hurry."

He didn't answer her.

"What color ribbon would you like this week?"

Annoyed, he said, "It doesn't matter. Just pick one."

He paced back and forth at the counter.

"Well, pink it is today." She went to the register and rang up the price. "That will be $7.50."

"Okay, okay." He took out his wallet and handed her his money.

"Here you go," she said, handing him two quarters.

He left the flower shop without saying anything back to her.

Ruth giggled to herself and shook her head. Every week that summer, Fred would come in for a dozen red roses. He was always in a hurry and a man of few words. In fact, almost no words. She wondered where he went every week with these roses. She smiled and said out loud to herself, "That girl sure is lucky to have a man who loves her so much that he buys her roses every week!"

Ruth had moved to the area from Ohio. She had relatives in Ford Heights. They owned a flower store and asked her to come and work for them. Looking for an adventure, she said yes. Ruth was friendly and quickly became a customer favorite. She had taught herself about flowers, and her family was teaching her the floral business.

She dreamed of owning her own flower shop one day. She loved the joy she felt in making beautiful floral arrangements, and she reveled in the delight her work brought to customers.

The scene went dark in my mind. *What was I meant to learn?* I instantly liked Ruth. She was an unassuming young woman, with a positive attitude that was infectious. I wrote down in my notebook all of my observations about Ruth, the flower shop, and—of course—my Uncle Fred.

When I closed my eyes again to rest them, a new scene played out. I could feel an autumn chill in the air. Ruth was getting the store décor ready for the upcoming season. The mums and pumpkins were filling the stockroom. As she was bringing them out to put them on display, she was startled by a man waiting at the counter.

"Oh, Fred, I didn't hear you come in. I haven't seen you in a while. What's it been? Almost a year?"

He nodded and said, "Yeah, yeah, I am in a hurry. I need a dozen red roses in a vase."

"Sure. A vase? Is it a special occasion?"

He didn't answer.

She thought he didn't hear her, so she repeated her question, louder this time.

He still didn't answer. He wasn't usually very talkative, but she felt like something seemed wrong.

"Are you okay, Fred?" she asked him.

"I just need roses, alright!" he barked.

"Okay. I will get you twelve red roses in a vase. Right away!" As soon as her back was turned, she rolled her eyes and headed to the flower cooler to pick out the roses.

Ruth returned in just a couple minutes and rang up his order. "That will be $9.00."

"$9.00?" Fred seemed surprised. "It's usually $7.50. When did the price go up?"

Softly, she replied, "I have to charge you for the vase."

"Okay," he grunted. "Do you have a card I can put with these? I need a card."

A card? she thought. *That's new. Maybe he has a new girlfriend.* "Here you go." She handed him a small white card and envelope. He grabbed a pen, scribbled something quickly in the card, and left in a huff.

Ruth followed him to the door. She locked the door behind him. It was time to close the shop for the day, and she worried he might come back for something else. She'd had enough of "Red Roses Fred" for the day.

The flower shop worked with the local funeral homes. In fact, they were the biggest customers of the store. Doing funerals was not Ruth's favorite assignment. The money was good, though. And Ruth learned that in a family business, you need to take in all kinds of work to pay the bills.

James was the funeral director's assistant. He was sweet on Ruth. Whenever possible, he would come into the flower shop to place his orders with Ruth. He liked her friendliness and hoped she liked him too.

A few days after her run-in with Fred, Ruth greeted James with a big smile and a friendly hello. James told her he had a funeral coming up and needed to place an order. He told her that a young woman had been found murdered recently. She was a young, pretty singer. She sang up the road from here, he told her, at the nightclub up on Dixie Highway. In a hushed tone, James concluded, "There are rumors she had a fan who was stalking her."

As Ruth listened to the details, she was feeling uncomfortable. "That poor woman," she said. She shuddered at the details of the story.

James loved sharing gossip, and he could tell he had Ruth's attention, so he continued, "I heard this fan is a local guy. The bouncer at the club told my buddy that some nut job would bring her flowers every week."

"He brought her flowers every week?" Ruth felt queasy. "Were they dating?"

"I don't think so. I heard he was following her. He liked her, but she didn't care too much for him. I even heard," James looked around and lowered his voice, "that he roughed her up one night."

"Well, I am going to pray for her and her family." Ruth was uncomfortable with the story. She wasn't sure how much of it was true. After all, she knew James was a bit of a gossip and a show-off. She asked him for the rest of the order to change the subject.

That evening, Ruth could not get the story James had told her out of her head. Even if it wasn't entirely true, the thought of a single woman being stalked and murdered left her unsettled.

She only had two days to deliver the flowers to the funeral home. The family had requested a huge bouquet of daisies. Ruth thought daisies seemed like an odd choice for a funeral. She called James to confirm that the order was correct.

"Yes, that's it. The girl I told you about? Her name was Daisy."

Hmm, she thought. *That would make sense. Daisies for Daisy. Very sweet.*

Ruth cried while she arranged the large vase of daisies. She felt compassion for this woman and her family. She wondered about the woman named Daisy. Ruth kept her word and prayed for them all. She wondered if Daisy hadn't been the object of Red Rose Fred's affections, but quickly put the thought out of her mind. What were the chances?

About a week later, a detective paid a visit to the flower shop. He had stopped in on Ruth's day off. When Ruth came in to work the next day, she found a note asking her to call Detective Roman at the Ford Heights Police Department. *Detective Roman*, she thought, rereading the note. She was confused. *Why would a detective want to talk to me?*

She reluctantly dialed the number. He asked if he could come by the shop and ask her a few questions about a recent case.

Ruth agreed, and she felt a rush of nausea. She felt suddenly dizzy and held onto the counter, afraid her legs might give out on her. About thirty-five minutes later, an older man in a tan trench coat and grey fedora came in. Ruth thought to herself, *This must be the detective. He doesn't look like he's buying flowers today.*

Detective Roman introduced himself. He explained there had been a murder recently in the area. A young woman was found dead in a cornfield not far from Ford Heights. He wanted to ask Ruth a few questions. Ruth nodded.

Detective Roman showed Ruth a picture of a woman. "This is Daisy. She was a singer in a nightclub not far from here."

Ruth said, "She's very pretty, but I've never seen her before."

The detective nodded. He explained that the police suspected she was being stalked by a man. The man may have killed her.

"Oh," Ruth swallowed. She didn't like where this conversation was going. "Well, what do you need from me, sir?"

"Miss, I think the man may have been buying her flowers from this store. Red roses to be exact."

Ruth gasped, "Red roses? Did you say red roses?"

He nodded, "Yes, red roses. Do you know anything that might help me solve this case?"

"Maybe." She lowered herself down onto the stool behind the counter. "There was a man, a man named Fred. He bought a dozen red roses every week. Every week. He stopped coming. I figured they broke up. Or she married him," Ruth quipped. Then she felt all the blood drain from her face. "But then he came back one more time. Just recently."

"What did he look like? This man named Fred. What did he look like?"

Ruth was having trouble describing hm. "Well, he was short, thin, and dark brown—I mean—he had light brown hair. Dark eyes. Quiet. Not very friendly." She started to tremble. She wanted to cry but the tears would not come.

"Do you know the man's last name?" the detective asked.

"No. We called him 'Red Roses Fred,' but I don't know his real name." She looked horror-stricken.

The detective tried to comfort her, "Take a deep breath. Do you need some water? Is anyone here with you?"

She was trying to think, *Was anyone there with her?* "No. No one."

"What time does the store close?"

"In about an hour?" Ruth was trying to compose herself. She was clearly shaken.

"Will you come to the station and answer a few more questions after work?"

"Sure. Of course."

After the detective left, the tears came. Ruth was overwhelmed with emotions—grief, shock, and mostly fear. She decided to close the store early. All the orders had been filled for the day, thank goodness. Ruth called home to tell her family she would be late for dinner. She didn't tell them why.

Driving over to the police station, Ruth replayed in her mind all the conversations she had with Fred about the roses. She remembered how uncomfortable he always seemed when she would tease him about his "lucky girl." He never really said much back to her. Ruth shivered at the thought that she could have been face-to-face with a murderer.

Detective Roman was waiting at the police station. He took her coat and offered her a cup of coffee. He asked a lot of questions. She didn't have many answers. She worried she wasn't being helpful enough. She assured him she was trying to help. He smiled and told her he knew she was.

As the questioning was winding down, the detective handed her a piece of a white card. He asked if she recognized the card.

She did. It was from her flower shop. "Look," she said, "that pink print is part of our shop's logo. See? Here." She pointed at the embossed metal name tag that was still on her dress.

He nodded. "That's what I thought. Do you think you could pick this Fred character out of a lineup?"

Ruth was suddenly afraid. She'd heard about lineups on television, and this felt like it was happening to someone else. She looked around the room and finally said, "I guess so. When?"

"I have to get a warrant and some other approvals, but I should be calling you in the next day or so. I really need your help, Ruth. We need to lock this guy up so he can't hurt anyone else."

Ruth agreed. She went home and straight to her bedroom. Her mind was reeling. She felt safe at home. She lay awake most of the night wondering about Fred and Daisy.

The next morning, Ruth popped out of bed and headed right to work. Her hope was to stay busy the next few days. That afternoon, while she was in the stockroom, she heard the bell ring and the front door open.

"Hello." The man's voice was soft but not friendly.

Ruth came into the shop and was stunned to see Fred.

"Oh, hi, Fred," she said. She tried to sound cheerful but could hear a quiver in her voice. "I haven't seen you in a while. You need some roses today?"

"Yes, a dozen red ones. And I will take them in a vase today. I'm seeing my girlfriend tonight. We are celebrating."

"Oh, well, that is nice," she said carefully.

"How have you been, Ruth?"

She wondered if he could sense her discomfort. He was oddly friendly towards her. She wondered if he knew she had been to the police. *He couldn't possibly know*, she quickly comforted herself. Ruth tried her best to stay calm and keep the conversation going with him.

As she finished arranging the flowers, she quickly showed him the bouquet and turned her back to ring them up the sale on the register.

"Wait, let me see," Fred interrupted.

She paused, almost frozen. This was the only time he had ever shown any interest in her work. Ruth showed him the vase quickly. She wanted him out of her store. She was all by herself in the shop today and suddenly feeling very vulnerable.

He handed her a ten-dollar bill. She tried to keep her hand from shaking while she made his change. As she handed him the dollar bill, he grabbed her hand.

She froze. He smiled and said, "Thank you, my dear Ruth."

When he left, she fell against the counter. She reached for the phone to dial the police station, but quickly changed her mind. She should wait for the detective to call her. That felt better to her.

The afternoon seemed to drag on. She kept looking at the clock, willing it to move faster. When closing time finally came, she grabbed her coat and purse and headed outside. She had parked behind the shop. As she put her key in the car door, she felt someone behind her. She spun around.

Fred was standing there. "Hi, Ruth."

She stammered hello back.

"I heard a friend of mine came to see you recently. He works at the police station. You might know him."

"No. No, I don't know any police officers."

"Oh, I think you do, Ruth. Get in the car. We need to have a little talk."

"No. No, we don't," Ruth insisted. "I need to be getting home. My family is waiting for me."

"I said get in the car, Ruth." He opened the door and pushed her in. Fred shoved her over to the passenger seat and wrested the keys from her hand.

They struggled. She yelled out, "Leave me alone. I don't know anything about you and Daisy."

Rage turned his eyes black. He shouted, "Daisy! Don't ever say her name again. Do you understand me?"

He grabbed both of Ruth's wrists and quickly tied them with a rope. He pulled so tight that the fibers cut into her skin. Ruth tried fighting him off. She wondered why no one was passing by. She needed help and kept crying out, hoping someone passing by would hear her.

Fred was strong and forceful. He shouted at her to shut up and to stop talking about Daisy and the roses. Ruth could not understand what he was saying. All she could manage to say was "Stop, please stop. You are hurting me."

But Fred didn't stop. He didn't care what she was saying. He had one job, and that was to eliminate the threat. He had no choice but to kill Ruth. She must be stopped. She knew too much. She had to die. Fred kept repeating those words. "She must be stopped. She knows too much. She must die." He pulled a longer piece of rope out of his pants pocket and tried to slip it around her neck.

With her hands tied together, Ruth knew she was trapped. She kept throwing her body from side to side, trying desperately to fight off Fred's attack. Her screams got louder. She desperately needed someone to notice their struggle. As her body weakened, she tried biting at him. But she was no match for the scrappy boxer and determined killer. The more she fought back, the more aggressive and determined he became.

Exhausted, she felt her head fall back on the passenger door's arm rest. In a split second, Fred slipped the rope around her neck and pulled with all his might. In a matter of seconds, Fred had eliminated the threat Ruth posed to him.

He waited for a few minutes to make sure she was dead. He pulled the rope one last time. Her body slipped down from the seat and dropped onto the passenger-side floor. If Ruth's family really was waiting for her, Fred needed to move quickly. He sat up, smoothed his hair back in place. He scanned the empty parking lot to make sure no one was watching.

Fred got out of Ruth's car and ran to his own. He parked it next to Ruth's passenger-side door. Fred opened his trunk. He retrieved Ruth's body from the floor of her car, then dumped her limp body into the trunk of his. He pulled a gray flannel blanket over her body before slamming his trunk shut.

Fred dashed back to Ruth's car. Inside, he carefully inspected the front seat and floorboards. He had to make sure he didn't leave anything of his behind. Once he was sure the front seat was clear, he returned to his own car. Looking over the parking lot one last time, he thought to himself, *Gotta cover my tracks*.

Fred drove home carefully, minding the speed limit and obeying all the traffic signals. He could not afford to be stopped by the police with a dead woman in his trunk. He whispered to himself, "She had to be stopped. She knew too much. She had to die."

Half a block from his mother's driveway, Fred turned off his headlights. He backed into the driveway slowly. Fred walked the perimeter of his car, looking in all directions to make sure he had not been followed home. Once he was sure he was alone, he opened his trunk. He wrapped the old, flannel blanket around Ruth's body, scooped her up, and carried her to the backyard.

The evening before, Fred had dug a grave for Ruth in his mother's backyard. He dropped her body into the shallow grave. Then, he grabbed the shovel he had propped up against the house. He wasted no time filling the hole with dirt.

Fred reached into his pocket and pulled out a round, flat rock. With his pocketknife, he etched an R on one side of the rock. He placed the rock at the end of her grave. Seeming satisfied with himself, he looked over a few feet to the right of Ruth's grave. He smiled to himself as he stared at the ground.

In the moonlight, he could see a stone similar in size to the one he had engraved for Ruth. He bent down and ran his thumb over the N he had etched in the stone. *My trophies.*

Fred picked up his shovel. He walked to the small garage and put it inside, along the wall. In the darkness, Fred made his way to the side door of his mother's house. He opened the door as quietly as he could.

His mother yelled out to him, "Fred, is that you? Where in the hell have you been?"

Fred closed his eyes and took a deep breath before he stepped inside.

—Chapter 10—
Along Came Polly

I was feeling restless. For months, I had worked tirelessly, pushing myself in my medium skills to connect with souls on the Other Side. While the work was rewarding, it also left me exhausted and disconnected from my family and friends. I had entered into a zone. I felt like my only way out was to solve these cases.

In the last year, I had met Teddy, Natalie, Daisy, and recently Ruth. But who was Polly? I had heard her name whispered to me so many times. Detective Roman also mentioned her. He confirmed that she was connected for a short time with my uncle. He also said that she wasn't Fred's type, which aligned with my sense of her.

Sitting in my office with an open notebook, I asked myself aloud, "Am I ever going to connect with Polly?"

I heard a women's voice say very clearly, "Yes, you are. There is more to unravel and definitely much to explore."

"Polly, are you really here, now?"

"Yes. Yes, I am, and I am here to assist and guide you. We will take it slow."

"Thank you," I said, relieved by her presence.

I felt her smile at my response. She said, "So you must have a lot of questions for me, Lynn?"

I answered cautiously, "Well, yes and no. I am not sure I want to keep going with this work. I am tired. The stories are heartbreaking and leave me unsettled. I want to bring the truth to light. I've always been seeking the truth. I'm just not sure I can keep going. I'm tired. I miss my life. I know that is probably a selfish thing to say, knowing what has happened to all the women I've met."

She smiled at me and said, "Lynn, you can do this work. This work is your life's work. You are the truth. You are bringing the truth to the world. You are bringing light to the darkness. The truth is healing. Not just for the families, but you are healing the world too. This is much bigger than you. One day, you will see the impact of this work. Trust the process. Trust yourself. Trust the divine timing of the unfolding."

Oh geez! There we go again with the unfolding! My least favorite word during the last year.

I sensed Polly wink at me. "I know. I know how you feel about that word. That is how this has been going, though. You know that, right?"

I nodded. Of course, I did.

"Lynn, it is just like before: one woman at a time. There is no rush. There really isn't. I want you to remember you have seen my body. Right by the canoe. Yep, that was me. Beth showed you. I got hit over the head with a shovel while my back was turned. I know now, they were both evil people. Very evil. Don't worry, I spooked them both often over the years. He was not a nice man, but I do believe his mother was worse. They left a lot of problems for people. Your aunt was a saint. He sucked the life out of her. She was dead inside by the end. She never felt peace."

Oh, I hated hearing that, even though I knew it was true. *I know, I know. I could see no life in her eyes. They were pitch black. No light at all. She was angry and sad until her death.*

"Yep, he took all the life from her. She left everything behind to be with him, hoping for a better life. She had no idea the torture that was ahead for her. She lived like a prisoner most of her life. He controlled everything—and I mean everything. She was stuck, you know? She really admired

143

how you spoke your mind and how you defended her to him. She felt your loyalty. Sleep well tonight, child. We will work more tomorrow."

"Okay, thank you, Polly," I said. *How will I ever fall asleep? I have so many questions to ask her.*

I did sleep that night. In fact, it was the first restful sleep I'd had in a long time. Connecting with Polly had been a huge relief, and it had also cleared some negative energy I had built up for myself around self-doubt.

I woke up the following morning to the most amazing sunrise! The sun was a bright, glowing ball of dark orange that rose slowly up through the dark, leafless trees behind our home. The sky was mesmerizing. I loved standing in the glow of it, stating my intention and gratitude for the day. I have seen this sunrise many times. But on this day especially, it was absolutely perfect. I took a picture of it so I would remember the moment.

When I sat down with my morning coffee, I opened up my notebook to a fresh page. I said aloud, "Okay, Polly, whenever you're ready!"

I felt a surge of powerful energy wash over my body. I immediately tasted cigarettes and wrinkled my nose. "Polly, what should I know about you? Where should we start? Where does your story start?"

"My *story*? That's a laugh!" she said, sarcastically. "I had a sad life. My mother died giving birth to me. My father was an alcoholic who couldn't hold a job. I bounced around from one relative's house to the next. Most of my life, I never felt wanted. I had an older brother, but he ran away many times. We got split up into different homes, so we never bonded. I think he ended up in jail. At least, that's what I was told. No one expected much from me, and I guess I never expected much from myself either."

"I am sorry to hear that," I said sincerely. "Your early life sounds like it was difficult."

"Yes, it really was. I felt like an outcast. I never felt loved. It was hard for me to trust people. I had to go to work at a young age."

"What did you do for work?"

"I worked in factories mostly. My favorite job was when I worked at an automotive stamping plant. We made parts for pickup trucks. The job paid well, and I worked the afternoon shift. I was uncomfortable around people, so it was perfect for me. I was a loner. It was hard to make friends. I had trust issues. It makes sense, right?"

I nodded. *It did make sense.* "Tell me more, Polly."

"Well," she hesitated, "I don't think you will think this is weird, because of your situation."

"My situation?" I was confused.

"I mean, your ability to talk to souls on the Other Side."

"Oh … *that* situation," I smiled.

"I was able to talk to my dead mother," she confided.

"That must have been nice."

"Not as nice as having her in person would have been. But it was better than nothing, you know. She would come to me, well her spirit would come to me at night. We had long talks. It was normal for me. I made the mistake of telling my cousin. She told her parents, and they thought I was crazy. They sent me to live with a different set of relatives. I bounced around a lot. I stopped telling people about talking to my mother at night. You are the first person I have shared that with in a long time." Polly was someone who needed a friend, even now.

"Are you with your mother now?" I asked.

"Yes, I am. We are together."

"I am glad for that," I said. "So tell me, how in the world did you meet my uncle?"

"Lynn, I met a lot of 'uncles.'"

"Oh." I could feel my face blush, knowing what she meant.

"I was looking for love in all the wrong places. I had a bad run of mean boyfriends. I am sure I attracted them because I was lost and broken. I was a bum magnet. I met your uncle when I was recovering from another bad relationship. I would sit in the park by the stamping plant before work. I did that every day before my shift started. I would smoke about ten cigarettes before I clocked in to work."

"Ten cigarettes?" My face contorted again. "Yuck!"

"I know, I know. If dating Fred hadn't killed me, the cigarettes probably would have done me in."

***

Every day before her shift at the stamping plant, Polly sat on a nearby park bench and loaded up on nicotine. One day, she noticed a man who let his gaze linger on her as he walked through the park. He was a clean-cut guy. Polly thought he looked like Howdy Doody. She wondered what he was looking at.

Polly noticed him again the next day. And the next. This went on for several weeks. He didn't speak to her. He seemed to be checking her out. He definitely wasn't Polly's type, and she couldn't imagine that she was his. But one day, he flashed a shy smile her way. Polly found herself blushing a bit.

The next day, he approached her. "I noticed you're out here a lot. Why's a pretty girl like you always sitting by yourself?" he asked.

Nobody had ever called her pretty before. Polly was torn. On the one hand, this guy sounded phony. But the allure of his compliment was more than she could resist. She smiled, despite herself. "I'm just getting ready for my shift at the plant," she explained.

"What's your name? Mine's Fred."

"Polly."

"Well, maybe I'll see you around, Polly."

"Yeah, okay." Polly's tone was aloof. She couldn't figure out this guy's angle.

Every day after that, Fred was there in the park before Polly's shift. He would sit and talk with her for a few minutes. He started to bring her little sweet treats—cookies and candy. Polly decided she had misread him at first. He was actually quite charming and even a little funny. Still, he seemed like a goody-two-shoes. Polly was used to dark and troubled guys, and Fred seemed different. She started to enjoy the attention. At work, she would pass the time with daydreams of going on a date with Fred.

Polly decided Fred was too shy to make her dreams a reality. She finally got up the nerve to ask him one day, "Fred, why don't you ask me out some time?" Fred seemed stunned as she handed him her phone number. Polly excused herself. It was time for her shift, and she had to clock in. She looked back over her shoulder to see Fred putting her phone number in his pocket.

After Polly's bold move with Fred, he disappeared. Polly figured she had probably scared him off. Every day for several weeks, she looked for him at the park, regretting her decision to be so forward. *A nice guy finally gives me the time of day,* she thought, *and I mess up my one shot at real happiness.*

Once in a while, Polly thought she saw Fred drive by the park in his car. Just when she'd stop thinking about him, she'd catch a glimpse of him near the park. She thought it was just her imagination reminding her what a fool she'd been.

About a year after she'd last spoken with Fred, she received a call from him on a Sunday afternoon. She didn't recognize his voice at first. When she realized who it was, she was a bit surprised. When he invited her to join him for dinner the following Sunday, she was stunned. But the date itself was the most shocking of all.

When Fred picked Polly up at her place, she asked, "So, where are we going?"

"To my mother's," Fred answered.

Polly thought this had to be a joke. No man in his right mind would take a girl to meet his mother on their very first date! She laughed out loud, "Oh, okay. But where are we really going?"

"We're going to my mother's," Fred deadpanned. He clearly wasn't joking. He looked hurt by Polly's teasing.

Polly realized her mistake. "Well, that sounds nice then." She tried to recover her light-hearted tone but the mood in the car had already turned sour.

When they arrived, Fred held the door open so Polly could enter the house first. Then, standing behind Polly at the threshold to the sitting room, Fred gestured to his mother, "Polly, I'd like for you to meet my mother, Mrs. Federoski. Mother, this is Polly."

"How do you do?" Polly said, trying her best to match Fred's formal tone and clean-cut demeanor.

"Hmph," Alma Federoski scoffed from the sofa, not even bothering to look away from the television.

"We'll eat after the nightly news," Fred explained to Polly. He gestured toward an upholstered, upright chair in the corner. Polly sat down, scooting over as far as she could to make room for Fred. Fred sat down on the sofa, next to his mother.

As soon as the news program ended, Fred stood up and led Polly to Alma's tiny kitchen. Polly was surprised to see a pot of hot food simmering on the stove. She hadn't smelled anything cooking when she entered the house. Fred offered Polly a plate of something gray and sloppy. It might have been chicken and dumplings, but the dish was so bland and awful, Polly didn't want to make any assumptions. Still, she didn't want to offend Fred or his mother, so she dutifully cleared away the serving she'd been given. She was relieved not to be offered a second helping.

Polly found it odd that no one spoke to her during the meal. Fred and his mother exchanged a few words about mundane topics, such as the grocery list and an upcoming appointment with a doctor. They gave Polly no invitation to speak, and she wouldn't have had anything to say if they had.

After dinner, Alma rose from the table without another word and headed back to watch television. Fred cleared the dirty dishes from the table, adding them to a pile already taking up residence in the kitchen sink. Then he smiled at Polly and gave a small jerk of his head toward the sitting room.

Polly found herself back in the uncomfortable chair, while Fred watched television next to his mother on the couch. No one spoke for the next two hours. At nine o'clock, Fred stood up and said to Polly, "Well, we'd better get you home then."

Polly had been on a lot of dates, but never one like this! She didn't know what to say to Fred on the way home. He filled the drive talking about his work as a salesman and the time he'd spent in the service. He spoke as though the evening had been perfectly normal.

For several weeks in a row, Fred called Polly to invite her to dinner. When the invitation was for a Sunday, Polly knew she was in for an awkward evening of eating bland slop in silence, followed by a couple hours of watching Fred and Alma watch television.

On rare occasions, Fred would take her out on a Friday or Saturday night. They would go to dinner and then to a local dance club. Fred didn't dance much, and Polly thought the scene was a drag. Still, Fred was nice enough and seemed to enjoy Polly's company. Who was she to complain?

Polly asked him one night, "Fred, why do you still live with your mother? I mean, you've got a great job. Don't you want more privacy?"

Fred bristled. "What's that supposed to mean?"

"I don't mean anything by it," Polly tried to smooth things over, "I'm just curious, is all."

"I can't imagine leaving Mother there all by herself," Fred began. He told Polly a long story about his father being abusive to his mother. Some of the details didn't make sense to her. Polly wondered how much of the story was true. She tried to ask a question, but Fred became very defensive.

"I don't expect you to understand," he spat. "I'm the man of the house. It's my job to take care of her, try to make up for all that."

Polly decided to drop the subject. It wasn't worth fighting about, and Fred probably had a good reason for being guarded. Yet Polly couldn't shake the feeling that she was dating both Fred and his mother. It was clear to Polly that Alma didn't care for the arrangement.

At dinner one Saturday night, Fred broke the news to Polly. "Mother says I can't see you anymore," he told her.

Polly threw her head back in laughter. But the joke was on her. Fred continued, "Mother says you're a hussy. She says you're no good for me. I can't see you again."

Polly was furious. She had finally found a nice man—one who liked her. Just her luck, this guy was too much of a coward to stand up to his own mother. Polly left the restaurant in a huff, walking the short distance back to her apartment. She poured herself a shot of cheap booze. And then another. She decided she was going to give Alma Federoski a piece of her mind.

Polly drove over to Alma's house. Fred's car was already back in the driveway. She charged up to the front door and knocked three or four times. Fred answered the door, but only opened it a crack. He said hello and asked what she was doing there.

"I really like you, and I think you probably like me, too," she told him. "And if you can't stand up to that woman, then I intend to!"

Fred's mother was not far behind him, yelling at him to shut the door. Fred waved his mother away. Polly took that as a sign he wanted to see her. Fred poked his head out the door for a moment and whispered, "I'll call you later, okay?" Polly nodded and stumbled back to her car.

Fred showed up a few days later at the park. He told Polly that his mother was upset about him seeing her. He promised he would find a way to make things work for everyone and asked Polly to be patient.

Time passed. Polly's patience ran out, and she went back to the life she knew. Polly worked hard and played hard. She dated lots of men, and they were nothing like Fred. Rough guys who drank and gambled. Guys who didn't take her home to meet their mothers.

Polly occasionally noticed Fred was following her. She refused to acknowledge him. *His loss*, she thought. *No guy should choose his mother over his girl, and no mother should expect it either.* At first, Polly liked knowing he was following her. It meant he still cared for her.

But something changed along the way. Fred started showing up everywhere Polly went. When Polly would go on dates, she'd look up from her meal to see Fred glaring at her from a nearby table. He wasn't subtle about it. In fact, he went out of his way to be a nuisance.

More than once, he tried to pick fights with Polly's companions. Polly wanted to confront him and demand he stop following her. But she decided it was better to avoid confrontation. Secretly, a part of her liked that he still gave her his attention.

During her shift one night, Polly was pulled off the line to take an urgent phone call. Phone calls were typically not allowed at the factory. Polly thought perhaps someone in her family had died. She answered the call with tremendous anxiety. It wasn't her family; it was Fred.

"I need to see you right away," he whispered into the phone.

"Fred, I'm working. Just taking this call is going to get me into trouble."

"Just come outside on your next break. I'll be waiting. I love you, Polly, and I need to see you," he begged.

I love you. No man had ever said those words to Polly. Her heart was fluttering, and she felt her face blush. As she hung up the phone, her supervisor asked if everything was okay. Polly giggled and said that everything was just fine. She was on Cloud Nine. She watched the clock, agonizing over every second that passed until her break.

When Polly stepped outside, Fred was waiting with a beautiful bouquet of flowers. He kissed her sweetly and offered an apologetic hello. He was sorry for breaking things off with her, he said, and had a plan for them to leave town and start a new life together. Polly was so excited. This was what she had dreamed of! She wanted to get as far away from the factory as she could. Starting a new life with a man who loved her sounded like the perfect plan.

The next day, Fred met Polly at the park before her shift. He told her to pack a suitcase that night, promising to pick her up when she got off work the next day. They would leave town together. She didn't ask him where they were going. She didn't care. She just wanted to start a new life.

Polly punched out for her final shift at the stamping plant. She didn't tell anyone she wasn't coming back. Fred was waiting by her car. He moved her suitcase from her back seat to his trunk.

"We'll send for your car later," he promised.

Polly said, "Yeah, okay," but she couldn't understand why they'd bother coming back for her old junker.

Once Polly got settled into the passenger seat, Fred told her, "I need to stop at my mother's house one last time before we leave town. There's something there I forgot to get." Then, seeing her tense up at the mention of his mother, he added, "Don't worry. Mother will fast asleep at this hour. She won't even know we were there. It'll only be a minute."

As Fred pulled up to his mother's house, Polly noticed a sinking feeling in the pit of her stomach. Fred turned off his headlights. He parked the car at a neighbor's house next door. He seemed anxious.

"Just have to grab a lug wrench from the garage. In case we get a flat. I left it in there a few days ago. Be right back."

Fred hesitated. He could see Polly was nervous to sit in the car by herself. The night was pitch black. Fred leaned across the front seat and kissed Polly on the cheek. "Would you rather come with me?" he asked.

Fred got out of the car and came around to open Polly's door. He held out his hand to help her out of the car. They walked together to the side of the garage. Fred squeezed Polly's hand and locked eyes with her. He put his index finger to his mouth, motioning for her to be quiet. Then he released her hand. "Just be a minute," he said and stepped into the garage.

Just as she lost sight of Fred, Polly felt something heavy smash into the back of her head. She fell face down on the ground, unconscious. Again and again came the heavy blows against the back of her head. Polly bled to death while she was dragged across the backyard, toward the canoe. Within moments, her body was kicked into a freshly dug hole.

Fred emerged from the garage to see his angry mother holding a shovel. He looked around for Polly, but she was nowhere to be seen. The blood drained from Fred's face.

"Mother! What have you done?" he demanded.

Alma walked past him without saying a word. When she reached the back door, she turned to face him. "I did what you could not do, Son. I took care of it," she said calmly. She went into the house like nothing had happened.

"Mother! Mother, what have you done? What have you done?" Fred paced in the backyard. He held head in his hands and shouted out into the black night sky. Then he knelt by the shallow grave where his dear Polly lay.

"I'm sorry Polly. I am. I didn't know. I wanted to run away with you. I did. I really did. We were going to be so happy. Just me and you. No one else. I love you. I love you. I am so sorry." Fred collapsed next to the grave in a fit of grief. His head rested on his knees. His shoulders shook as he sobbed.

Watching her son cry over some floozy kept Alma in her fury. She listened for a while, occasionally letting out a derisive snort. When she thought his crying had gone on long enough, she rapped on the window with her hand. Shaking her head in disgust, she raised the window and yelled out to him, "Enough, Frederick. Enough with this foolishness! Stop crying over that two-bit hussy. I told you she was not good enough for you. She was not your kind. Now, I've made this easy for you. Finish the job." With that, his mother slammed the window shut.

It took Fred awhile to regain his composure. He searched in the darkness for the shovel, which his mother had dropped near the driveway. His sorrow turned to anger as he returned to Polly's final resting place. His rage increased with each shovel full of dirt. *Finish the job,* he told himself. And he did.

Fred propped the shovel against the back of the house. He charged through the back door and went in to confront his mother. She was watching the tv with the volume turned down low. He was annoyed to find her half asleep.

"Mother!" he shouted.

She jumped and sat up fully awake. "What?" she snapped.

"How could you? How could you? How could you kill my girl? Why, Mother? Why?" he demanded.

Alma was not accustomed to her son standing up to her, and she certainly did not appreciate his disrespect. Standing up slowly, she walked toward him with fire in her eyes. "Don't you ever, *ever* talk to me with that tone in your voice again. Do you hear me?" Not letting him answer, she kept charging at him. Fred inched backward, stopping when his back hit the sitting room wall. Fred was trapped.

Alma looked up into his face, "I told you. I did what you should have done. That girl was trouble, and you know it. You thought you were going to run away with *her*? Sneaking out with your packed suitcase in the night! Thinking you were going to leave me again? Leave *me?* How dare you!"

Fred pushed her away from him with all his might. Startled, his mother fell back onto the couch. He slammed the back door open and stormed to his car, still parked in the neighbor's driveway. He sped off, his car tires squealing into the night. Fred didn't know where he was going or if he would be back.

—Chapter 11—
Putting the Pieces Together

On a Monday, after my morning meditation, I organized the notes and folders on my desk. One stack contained the eight worn manila folders from the police station. Each one represented an unsolved crime. And to me, each symbolized a failure on my part to solve the case.

The other stack of folders told a different story. The bright pink, green, yellow, and turquoise file folders seemed triumphant by comparison. Polly, Ruth, Natalie, and Daisy. Beneath those lay a pale lavender folder marked with an X and a blue-gray folder for Mrs. W.

I reached for my phone to call Karen at the Ford Heights Police Department. The moment I picked up the phone, I felt it buzzing in my hand. I cringed when I saw the "Unknown Number" from a Chicago area code. Probably someone trying to reach me about my car's extended warranty. Still, I felt the urge to answer the call.

"Hello, this is Lynn," I answered. I could hear the irritation in my own voice.

"Lynn, Bradley," said the voice on the phone.

"Beg your pardon?"

"Bradley here. I have news for you," he said.

"What great timing! I was just picking up the phone to call you!" I chimed. "I hope the news is good news?"

"Affirmative. We just closed Daisy's case. The Elgin lab found a match. Your uncle's DNA was found on the victim's clothing."

My eyes welled with tears. "That's fantastic!"

"Well, that's the good news," Bradley said.

"Is there bad news?" I asked hesitantly.

"Yes. After we got word from the state police, I requested a records search on your missing person case. Nothing at all on anyone named Polly or Natalie in the timeframe you gave us." Bradley almost sounded disappointed.

"That makes sense, actually. I've learned a lot more about Polly since we talked. She didn't have close family ties. The factory and her landlord probably assumed she just skipped town. Similar story for Natalie," I explained.

"Then we're chasing a ghost," Bradley said without irony.

"Not exactly," I cautioned. "I have another name for you to check."

Bradley seemed skeptical, but he heard me out as I gave him the highlights from my notes on Ruth. "Someone definitely would have been looking for her. Her family owned a flower shop in town," I concluded.

"I'll see what I can find," Bradley offered. "Can you bring your notes and meet me at the station next week?"

As I set down my phone, I heard Detective Roman's familiar voice say, "You did good, Kid."

***

When I stepped into the police station, Karen greeted me with a big smile. She said, "Lynn, we've been expecting you!" She winked and jerked her head ever-so-slightly to the right. Bradley had been waiting for me to arrive.

I followed Bradley past the small room that had been the spot of our first meeting. We headed to the large office in the corner, where Captain Simon sat waiting for us.

"Lynn! Great to see you again!" the captain said. "We thought maybe you'd forgotten about us."

"Not a chance," I smiled. "I've been busy, and I've learned so much. I have a lot to tell you." I pulled a dozen folders out of my bag. I divided the folders into two stacks and laid them on Captain Simon's desk, I noticed him eyeing the stack of police files.

"Shall we begin with the bad news?" I asked, sensing the question in his gaze.

Bradley looked puzzled.

"I can't solve these cases," I said, pointing to the beige folders, "… yet."

"What does that mean, exactly?" asked Bradley.

"My uncle didn't commit these murders. My sources tell me that, in time, I'll be able to help with all kinds of cases. But for now, I have to focus on the damage my uncle did while he was here on earth," I explained.

Bradley took a deep breath. "Your missing-persons cases," he said with a sigh.

"Yes," I confirmed. "I promise I'm not holding your cases hostage. I want to help with them, and I think I'm getting closer. But I have to clear this negative energy from my uncle before I can help these other souls."

I could see Bradley fighting the urge to roll his eyes. He was warming up to me personally, but he still thought I was a quack.

"Okay. So, what's the *good* news?" he asked.

"That depends. Did you find a missing-person report filed for Ruth?"

"In fact, I did," he admitted.

"Then the good news is, we can close her case!" I proclaimed.

"Talk to us, Lynn," said Captain Simon.

I picked up the small stack of brightly colored folders. Opening the green folder, I explained, "Ruth worked in a flower shop. She was a witness who could connect my uncle Fred to Daisy's murder. Fred killed her to keep her from talking. He buried her in his mother's backyard." Confirming that I had their attention, I relayed Ruth's entire story to the men.

"When you search for Ruth, you're going to find the remains of two more women," I said, then recounted Polly's story and Natalie's. "Polly wouldn't have had anyone looking for her. She lived alone and didn't have any family ties. Natalie was also a bit of a loner. She had a falling-out with her family and lived in the same boarding house as some of my uncle's other victims."

"We couldn't find anything on Natalie, though," said Bradley.

"I'm not surprised. The woman who ran the boarding house probably wouldn't have reported her missing. She'd had a run of bad luck with her tenants. Admitting that she'd lost a fourth girl would have destroyed her financially."

"It's a great story," said Bradley, "but we can't order an excavation of the property without any physical evidence."

I shot a pleading glance at Captain Simon.

"I'm sorry, Lynn, but Bradley's right," Captain Simon replied.

"In that case, I have one more idea," I said, pulling a copy of *Chicago Living Magazine* from my bag.

***

A few weeks later, I drove back to the Ford Heights lot that had been owned by Alma Federoski. With Karen's help, I learned that the house hadn't been sold at all. It had been seized by the city of Ford Heights due to a tax lien. Either Margie was mistaken about the sale or had been too embarrassed to tell me the truth.

The condemned house had finally been torn down, and I circled the block a few times before I realized I was in the right place. The now-vacant lot looked too small to have ever contained a house, a driveway, a detached garage, and an improvised graveyard. I tried to reorient myself while I waited for the rest of my team.

I pulled my phone out and scrolled through my pictures. I found some photos I had taken of the house a couple years earlier. I held the phone at arm's length to match the tree line from the photo to the tree line behind the lot. Then I noticed the apartment building—Teddy's apartment building—off to one side.

The driveway was still there, at least in part. I walked around the property in disbelief. The weeds that were as tall as the house were all gone, except for one row of them at the back of the lot. I assumed that was the property line. With the weeds cleared away, I realized that the canoe had also been removed. I tried to picture in my mind the spot where it had been. When I closed my eyes, I could see it perfectly, along with the gruesome secrets that lay beneath it. *I will tell your stories*, I silently promised the women who were buried there.

I was soon greeted by Nathaniel Chase, the journalist who had worked to uncover the truth about the Starved Rock murders, and his friend Dr. Curtis, an anthropology professor from a local university. They were accompanied by half a dozen college students, most of whom introduced themselves with nicknames like Keto, Shiny, and Biscuit.

Bradley and Captain Simon were the last on the scene. They brought with them a permit, allowing us access to the property. After brief introductions, the college students began setting up tripods and scientific equipment around the vacant lot.

"Can you explain exactly what we're doing here?" Bradley asked.

"Sure!" said Dr. Curtis. "These kids are students from the university—Anthropology department. They're going to scan the ground for anomalies using LiDAR and GPR. LiDAR stands for Light Detection and Ranging. Basically, it sends out pulses of light to measure small changes in the surface of the land. GPR is Ground Penetrating Radar. It's like sonar, but in the ground." She excused herself to help the students with their setup.

Bradley scrunched his eyebrows in thought. "I've read about that. GPR's pretty good for detecting shallow graves, right?"

"That's what we're hoping to find out," Nathaniel said, winking at me. "But as far as these kids know, we're just giving them a place to try out their equipment. We don't want to bias their data or analysis. If they don't find anything, no harm done. They get credit for a field project, and the city will know the lot is clear for future development."

"But…?" asked Bradley.

"But if they *do* find something suspicious, then we can request permission to dig a little deeper," Captain Simon interjected.

"Right!" I said, practically bouncing with excitement. "And Nathaniel will have another article to sell to *Chicago Living*."

We watched for the next couple of hours while the students took turns working with the equipment. Under Dr. Curtis's direction, they pushed buttons on what looked like a large camera atop a tall tripod. Then they each walked a couple laps back and forth on the lot, pushing something that resembled a walk-behind lawn mower. After they finished their initial scans, they huddled around a laptop to admire their data.

We saw a couple of the students point to the computer screen, then to a spot in what would have been the backyard. The girl who had introduced herself as Biscuit ran back to the van to grab another piece of equipment.

"And that one looks like a metal detector," I mused.

"I think that one *is* a metal detector," Nathaniel confirmed.

He made his way over to the group of students to ask about their findings. I followed him, reminding myself not to say anything that might bias the students' research.

"What can you see in the readings?" I asked carefully.

"Not much without some processing," the student called Shiny said. He pointed to some wavy lines on the screen. "We see some utility lines … here. Looks like there used to be a structure … there. And another one … there. Then some anomalies showed up where we didn't expect it … back here." Again, he pointed to the computer screen and then to a spot in the backyard, where Biscuit was sweeping the ground with the metal detector.

Shiny continued, "We'll have to run the data through some software to make sure. Should take about a week. Anyway, thanks for letting us use your place for field practice!"

I didn't correct his assumption about who owned the property. We turned our attention back to Biscuit, the young woman with the metal detector. After a few moments, she bent down to examine something on the ground. She picked up a small object, brushed the dirt off it, and shrugged. "I found it!" she shouted to her classmates and began walking back toward the group.

"What is it?" Keto asked.

"Just an old name tag," Biscuit said. "But at least we know the equipment works!"

I felt goosebumps on my arms. "May I see it?" I asked. She handed it to me, her interest in the trinket already fading. I turned the metal name tag over in my hand and scraped the dirt away with my thumbnail. My legs nearly collapsed beneath me. In one corner, I could make out an embossed rose. The remaining dirt stuck in the recesses where the letters had been engraved: *CONNER FLORAL. RUTH.*

—Chapter 12—
The Truth Finds Its Way

Just as they had promised, Dr. Curtis and her Anthropology students emailed their findings to us the following week. The surface measurements showed clear, rectangular depressions where the house and garage had been. The underground GPR scan didn't mean anything to me. It looked like wavy lines and static. The narrative portion of the report didn't offer much clarity.

Just as I was starting to feel frustrated, Nathaniel called.

"Oh, thank goodness! I can't make sense of this thing," I answered.

"Hey, Lynn. Hold on a second. I have Dr. Curtis on the other line. Merging the calls now," he said. A round of "hello"s and "can you hear me"s followed. Once we were all accounted for, Dr. Curtis explained the findings.

"If you line up the LiDAR image and the GPR image, you can see how the wave pattern changes in spots. You can see where the structures had been. The house had a basement. And then, in the backyard, we see three relatively large anomalies in the ground density. Several traces of metal in the middle anomaly. One or two traces of metal in the other spots, and a bit more off to one side."

"What do you think those spots are?" I asked, unsure about whether Nathaniel had given Dr. Curtis the whole story.

"They are consistent with clandestine graves. It looks like you've found them, Lynn," she said.

I guess she knew what we were looking for. "I'm so relieved! What happens now?" I asked.

"We'll brief your friends at the Ford Heights Police Department about our findings. This should be enough for them to order an excavation."

"Thank you so much!" I practically shouted into the phone. "I *knew* they were there. I knew the truth would find its way."

About an hour later, I got a call from Bradley, confirming that they would file paperwork for a search warrant. Even though we couldn't bring the women back to life, Bradley and I shared a moment of triumph. Discovering the answers and filling in the missing pieces to solve the cold cases was satisfying, albeit unsettling. Our work would provide answers to the victims' families. We hoped these answers would bring them closure and the long-awaited peace they had most likely prayed for over the decades. These beautiful souls deserved more of a life than they had been given.

I felt the presence of the women, celebrating the news with me. We all knew it was just a matter of time before their families would be notified that the cases had been solved. I smiled at the spirits and thanked them for trusting me with their stories.

After a quick prayer, I began packing up my notes and organizing my files after months of neglect. My filing was usually impeccable: labeled, color-coded, and alphabetized. Despite my spiritual gifts, I am truly a Type-A personality. I felt that clearing my space would also clear my head and my energy for what lay ahead. And I intended to keep my promise to Captain Simon. After a short break, it would be time to work on the captain's cold cases.

I began sorting bills and tax paperwork into their respective piles. Halfway through the first big stack, I noticed a document with Uncle Fred's name on it. Odd. I thought I'd filed all his papers more than a year before. As soon as I realized what I was holding, I yelled for Sam.

Sam stuck his head in my office just a few seconds later. He looked around at the paperwork mess and cringed. He was probably worried I was going to ask for his help.

"Don't worry. I got this. It's therapeutic," I explained.

"Oh, thank goodness!" he chuckled. "So, what's up?"

"Look what I found. It's a deed to an empty lot Uncle Fred owned."

"Where is it?" Sam asked.

"Ford Heights. Why would he buy an empty lot? What was he going to do with it? This doesn't make sense, does it?" I looked over to Sam, knowing of course he had no answers for my rapid-fire questions.

Sam shrugged. "Maybe he filled up his own yard and needed more space to hide bodies?" Sam didn't laugh, and neither did I.

"Oh, listen to this! He paid $32,890 for it in 1972. That seems like a lot of money for back then, right? I mean, there wasn't even a house on it. I think you could get a whole house for that kind of money in the seventies."

"You're right," Sam agreed. "How big was the lot? Maybe he was planning to build on it."

"Small. Less than three thousand square feet. Not even a tenth of an acre … Holy shit!" My hands began to shake.

"What?" Sam asked, startled at my sudden outburst.

"He bought it from a woman named Edith Wondolowski!" I practically shouted.

"Okay?" Sam wasn't following.

"Sam, it's Mrs. W. You know, from the boarding house. Some of the women lived there!"

My mind suddenly flooded with questions. *Why did she sell? And why did he pay so much for the lot? What was he up to?* Poor Sam just stared at me in disbelief.

"I have to call Bradley," I said. *So much for taking a break.*

About the Author

Author and self-taught medium D.L. Benning became spiritually curious after her father's murder in 1984. It would take twenty-five years for her father to start a conversation with her. Since then, Benning has sought out education and guidance to enhance her gift. She credits many teachers and kind souls from the Other Side for guiding her along the way.

Benning grew up in Central Illinois. Though she earned a teaching degree, she never taught in a classroom. She's spent the last three decades in Chicago, first selling steel, and later moving into Human Resources within the metal industry.

Benning has spent her adult life transforming her own trauma into initiatives that serve others. As a survivor of childhood sexual abuse, she created a program to help sex workers and victims of human trafficking. Benning later founded The Pink Bridge, a self-care community for women navigating adversity, after she beat breast cancer in 2011. Despite all she's been through, most people who know Benning say she's the most positive person they've ever met.

Benning currently lives with her husband in the Chicago suburbs. Her favorite job is being an aunt to fifteen nieces and nephews. She continues to use her medium gifts to channel stories for her readers.

Learn more about Benning's work at

www.ThePinkBridge.com

and

www.YourFriendsCameToSeeMe.com

—Book 1—
The Ford Heights Murders

Introducing investigative medium Lynn Monroe. Lynn is a self-taught medium who channels inspiration and affirmations for her blog. Her quiet life is thrown into disarray when her estranged and aging Uncle Fred insists that she take over his estate. Lynn's gifts as a medium soon reveal Uncle Fred's sinister past. Settling his affairs takes on new meaning when his departed victims seek Lynn's help in solving their decades-old murders.

The Ford Heights Murders **is available in paperback and on Kindle.**